The Devil's Kiss

She was a strange child. No one had ever seen one like her before. She was as swift and silent as the wind, as lithesome as a fawn, and as rare and beautiful as a bird of paradise. In her eyes burned all the passion of a summer's day.

To the decent, God-fearing people of Marie Regina, a small country village in southern England, she was a mystery, indeed!

And so she should be. For Willow Falcon, the illegitimate daughter of the future Lord Falcon, was no ordinary woman. On her thigh she bore a birthmark, a purple crescent, known to the superstitious peasants as the kiss of the devil! a symbol of supernatural powers. In her heart burned the hatred of an outcast, and with her evil power she brought the mighty Falcon family to its knees in a storm of bloody vengeance, treachery, and deceit.

Catherine Darby's
The Falcon Saga -5
Falcon Royal

POPULAR LIBRARY • NEW YORK

FALCON FAMILY DYNASTY

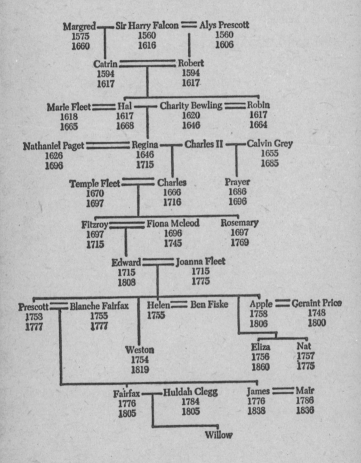

PART I
1818

Chapter 1

The stagecoach had made good time along the London road. It was now cresting the rise, above the gentle slope leading to the bridge. At the other side of the bridge the road sloped upward again, toward Maidstone.

The young woman in the corner adjusted her bonnet slightly so that its brim shaded her face even more. Every time she lifted her eyes she met the admiring gaze of the portly gentleman seated opposite. His attentions irritated her; she had spent most of the journey determinedly staring out of the window at the changing landscape.

Even a casual observer would have been distracted by the prettiness of her heart-shaped face with its delicate features and large eyes of so vivid a blue that even the whites of them seemed tinged with the shade. Tendrils of black, curly hair feathered her round, white forehead, and full, pink lips closed over small, gleaming teeth.

The recent death of her father in impoverished circumstances had made it necessary for her to seek a situation; Felice Browning was on her way to take up a post at *Kingsmead* as governess to the two children of Lord Falcon. Her mind went back to her interview with Lord Falcon in an inn near Temple Gardens the week before.

She had dressed carefully in the only good day gown she still possessed. That it was highly unsuitable for a young lady seeking employment as a governess never entered her head; she knew only that her reflection in the cheap mirror pleased her. The high-waisted dress of blue silk flattered her tall, slim figure, and the matching cloak was ruffled deeply at the hem. Her straw bonnet was trimmed with a spray of cream rosebuds and tied under her chin with blue silk.

She had walked from her lodging house to the inn, grateful that the fine spring weather had rendered the streets comparatively clean. Giving her name at the inn, she was conducted into a private sitting room at the back, where a tall gentleman with greying fair hair and blue eyes rose to greet her.

"Miss Browning? I am James Falcon." His voice was pleasant, his handshake firm.

"Yes, milord." She dropped a curtsey and sat primly on the edge of the chair he indicated.

"You seem very young," he observed, sitting down at a little distance.

"I am eighteen, sir."

"I was envying you, not criticizing," he said, smiling. "You say in your letter that this is the first time you have sought a post."

"I was at school until two years ago," she explained. "Then my mother died and I came back to London to be with my father. We lived in Chelsea."

"But you are not living there now?"

"My father had a . . . certain reverse of fortune, sir. We were forced to sell the house."

Her parents had lived in that Chelsea house all their married days on a small pension inherited from her grandfather. She believed they had been happy, but her mother had craved luxury and pretty things, and so the pension had frequently been wagered on horses and cocks and the spin of a coin. When, upon her mother's death she had returned home from school, it had been to a father already deep in debt, pathetically insisting that his luck was bound to change at any moment.

"My father was not—not a practical man," she confessed, twisting her hands together. "When he died last month, he left nothing."

"And you have only the one reference?"

"From my parish priest, yes. If you queried my former head mistress I'm certain she would also give a good account of my character, but I . . . I have not told her that I am seeking a post." Her delicate skin had flushed crimson. To have returned to her expensive school in the position of suppliant would have galled her pride unendurably.

"We are Anglicans, and there is no Catholic church at Marie Regina," he said, "but there is a small chapel some two or three miles distant where a priest comes once a month to say mass. You could attend there."

"Thank you, milord."

"Your Christian name is an unusual one," James Falcon commented.

"Felice was my grandmother's name, sir. My mother came from France at the start of the Terror. She was a de Reignet."

He understood now from whence came her dark,

delicate beauty, the faint air of elegant coquetry. "Do you speak French?"

"Yes, sir. My mother liked to speak it to me when I was little."

"It would be an asset if you were to teach it to my children. I see from your letter that you offer singing and embroidery, too."

"Yes, milord." She flushed again, in agony lest he should request her to perform, but he laced his fingers together and leaned forward slightly, saying earnestly, "As you may have gathered from the advertizement, my wife and I are seeking a governess for our two children. Nathan is ten and Joan is six. Up to now my wife has given them their lessons, but they are intelligent children and require more advanced instruction. Indeed, Nathan will be going away to school in a year or two, but he is somewhat delicate and we think it best to keep him at home for the present. Have you ever been to Kent?"

She shook her head, fascinated by his slow, pleasant voice.

"Marie Regina is a small village. It takes its name from an old monastery that used to stand on the hill beyond the river. It is only a ruin now. The monks were dispossessed in the sixteenth century and much of their land was given to an ancestor of mine. The main house, *Kingsmead*, was built then, though it has been added to since. There is a smaller manor house on the estate which came into the family through marriage, but it is unoccupied at present. We are a very quiet little community. There are not many gaieties for a young lady."

"Oh, I am not in the least gay," she assured him hastily. "My father disliked mourning and made me promise not to wear any for him. It is not frivolity which dresses me in blue."

"I am certain it is not." His glance was kind. "As to your duties, my wife will instruct you in those. The salary is twenty pounds a year, but you will require a small advance in order to settle your affairs here, I daresay."

"Then I am engaged?" The color surged up into her face again as he extracted five golden guineas from a leather wallet and handed them to her.

"And will, I hope, settle down very comfortably with us. We live very simply at *Kingsmead*. I think you will be happy there."

She had left the inn in a daze at her good fortune. The money in her purse would pay the rent she owed and secure her a seat on the Maidstone stage. Lord Falcon had given her a week in which to make ready, but she could hardly wait. She pictured herself reading to the two children, taking them for walks down leafy country lanes, hearing the slow, pleasant voice say, "I cannot imagine how we managed before you came to us." Of Lord Falcon's wife she did not think at all.

Cramped against the window, she watched the landscape unroll. The day was fine and warm, and for the past hour she had enjoyed the sight of apple trees in their full glory of May flowering.

The coach unexpectedly rolled to a stop and the coachman's face loomed at the glass. "Miss Browning? You wanted to be set down at the gates of *Kingsmead*."

"Oh, yes. Thank you." She stepped into the road and waited while her portmanteau was handed down to her. Then the coach rolled on in a cloud of dust, and she saw the face of the portly gentleman watching her disconsolately from the window.

She shook off the irritation he caused in her as she shook off the dust from the coach and looked about her with a mingling of curiosity and joyous anticipation. At the other side of the road the high-banked meadows rolled down toward a stone wall beyond which she could see a tall spire. On her left, iron gates opened to reveal a drive which wound between oak and elm trees. Their branches laced overhead to create the illusion of a cool, green tunnel.

Felice picked up her bag and began the long walk between the trees. The ground was well cared-for, and between the trunks she glimpsed the shoots of young wheat spearing the ground. Here and there sunlight filtered patchily through the entwined leaves, rendering the other spaces more shadowy.

Something was moving, keeping pace with her behind the trees. It flashed into view, briefly green, and then was gone again. She slowed her steps, but caught nothing except a faint rustle, and then the figure stepped out into the drive, stood poised for a moment, and darted away.

It looked like a child, she thought, or the dream of a child, a slim, green shape with a waterfall of pale hair. For a moment Felice felt cold, as if a wind had rushed through the leaf-ceilinged tunnel, and then common sense reasserted itself and, gripping her bag more firmly, she went steadily forward.

A stone wall reared before her, its façade interrupted by a rounded arch through which she glimpsed a cobbled yard. At the side of the arch a tree spread its branches against the wall. The leaves of the tree were large and rust-colored, veined in deep purple. Felice felt compelled to put out her hand and pull off a leaf. She had never seen such a tree before. When she crumpled the leaf, the scent of vinegar rose into the air.

After a moment, drawing a deep breath—for she was seized by an unaccountable nervousness—Felice walked through the arch into the courtyard. The house faced her, its chimneys rising up from the slate roof, its windows set deep in stone mullions. Creepers trailed like green spider's webs over the stone, and three shallow steps led up to the oaken door. It was an old and beautiful building, but for an instant the impulse to turn and flee was so strong that she shivered again and, for no reason, thought of the strange, green-clad figure who had come and gone so swiftly.

"Can I help you, miss?" A pink-cheeked maidservant in a print dress and mobcap had come around the corner of the house.

"I am Felice Browning. I believe Lady Falcon is expecting me."

Her voice came out timidly, but the servant smiled in a friendly fashion. "You'll be the new governess, miss. The stage made good time, then? I'll take your bag for you."

The girl went ahead briskly up the steps, the heavy door yielding to her solid push; Felice, relieved of her bag, her nervousness dispelled by a friendly face, followed at her heels.

The door opened into a high-raftered hall hung with faded tapestry. A few pieces of enormous furniture met her startled gaze, and then her eyes moved the length of the hall to the stone staircase that led up, past twin fireplaces, to a stone-railed gallery above.

"The mistress is in the solar," the maid said cheerfully. "I'll have Robert take your bag upstairs. Would you like to wash your hand, miss?"

"Oh, please, if you will be so kind as to tell me . . . er . . ."

"Betsy, miss. Nan, that's my sister, and I are the housemaids here. Robert and John do most of the other work between them." Her foot was on the lowest step when a door on the left opened and a voice said in peremptory accents, "Betsy! If Miss Browning is come, be good enough to bring her to me."

The owner of the voice had already turned her back and retreated into the other room. Betsy made a small, eloquent face and indicated mutely that handwashing must come later.

Betsy sprang up the stairs, rapped politely at her lady's door, pushed it wide and said primly, "If you please, milady, Miss Browning is come."

The room beyond was also panelled, its windows overlooking the courtyard. Felice's first thought was an indignant, "but she knew very well I am here, for she must have watched me from the window."

"Thank you, Betsy. You may bring hot water for tea and some sponge fingers. Miss Browning, be good enough to sit down. You must be tired after your journey."

"I was fascinated by the scenery, Lady Falcon."

Taking the proferred seat Felice studied her employer's wife with interest. Lady Falcon appeared to be in her early thirties, and was not pretty. Thin, faded, and sallow-skinned, her chestnut hair drawn back severely into a coiled plait, it would have been easy to dismiss her as negligible had it not been for the dignity of her bearing, the authority in her deep voice, and a peculiarly intense, almost passionate quality in her brown eyes.

"You look delicate," Lady Falcon said.

"Oh, but I am very strong," Felice said quickly.

"And very young." The brown eyes were critical.

"I am past eighteen, Lady Falcon, and I made no secret of my age when your husband interviewed me."

"You may address me as Lady Mair. We do not stand upon ceremony here. I must confess I would have preferred an older, more experienced person. Unfortunately I was unable to accompany my husband to London, for our son Nathan was suffering from a spring ague. Ah, here is Betsy."

The maid set down the heavy silver tray, bobbed another curtsey, and departed. Lady Mair rose, the loose folds of her dark red dress swirling about her, and reached for an elaborately painted caddy, unlocking it with a small key from the bunch at her waist. Slowly she spooned the tiny black leaves neatly into the pot. Not until the fragrant liquid had been poured into the cups, sugar and lemon passed, and the caddy relocked and returned to its shelf, did she resume her discourse.

"I understand you speak French, Miss Browning."

"Yes, milady. My mother was French."

"I am Welsh myself, but I have never spoken my native tongue with my children. French will be of more practical use." There was still a faint lilt in her voice, a flavor of mountains. Her hands lifting the cup were thin and muscular.

"I shall do the very best I can," Felice said. In a moment she would disgrace herself by bursting into tears, and then this unfriendly, brown-eyed woman would have the right to despise her.

"I am sure you will." Either Mair had repented her ill-humor or the tea had restored her temper, for she smiled in a friendly fashion which made her look much younger. "You will find your duties pleasant enough," she said. "We rise early and keep country times, with dinner at noon and supper at seven. We eat in the main hall then, but the children have their supper at six, and you will prefer to eat with them."

"Yes, milady." Felice drank her tea with great concentration.

"The children go down to the village for religious instruction from Mr. Penn on Wednesday and Friday mornings, and on two afternoons a week they ride with their father," Lady Mair was saying. "While they are out you will be at liberty to take what exercise you need. In the evening there is a certain amount of sewing to be done. My husband tells me you are a Catholic?"

"Yes, milady."

"We have no prejudice," Lady Mair said, "on condition you do not try to sway the children toward your beliefs. Mass is said in St. Mary's Chapel once a month, but on the other three Sundays I shall expect you to attend the village church with us."

"Yes, milady." It made little difference where she went; since her father's death, she had attended church out of habit, not conviction.

"The children are back from their ride." Felice had heard nothing, but Lady Mair's thin, vivid face had softened perceptibly and she rose with eagerness in her eyes as the door opened and a boy and a girl came in. They were good-looking children, with brown hair and blue eyes. The boy was thin for his age, as if he had outgrown his strength too rapidly. The girl was much smaller, with rosy cheeks and a lively, inquiring air.

"Mama, it is much nicer when Father takes us riding," the little girl exclaimed. "John will not allow us to gallop."

"John has no desire to be responsible for an accident," Lady Mair said. "Now, instead of bursting in like savages, make your greeting to Miss Browning."

The boy bowed gravely, but the little girl gave an excited skip crying, "Are you the governess? Are you? Are you, Miss Browning?"

"Yes, yes, I am."

"We're not fond of learning things," the little girl warned.

"Joan, hush!" The boy looked extremely embarrassed. "My little sister has no manners, Miss Browning."

"But she is truthful and that is important, too," Felice said.

"I might do some lessons for you, if you like," the little girl said generously.

"Children, that is enough." Their mother's voice was chidingly indulgent. "Miss Browning, this is Nathan and this is Joan, as you may have guessed."

"Can we show her the house?" Joan was demanding. "Can we, Mama?"

"If you wish." Lady Mair turned to Felice, her face still gentle, as if contact with her children brought out the best in her nature. "Two wings were added to the original building at different times. My husband is very interested in preserving the flavor of the past, so the main wing has been kept very much as it always was. He and I have our rooms above these; you and Joan will sleep on the other side of the house over the servants' quarters."

"I have a room in the east wing next to Uncle Weston," Nathan volunteered.

"My husband's bachelor uncle lives with us," Lady Mair explained. "He spends most of the day in his own apartment, embroidering." Her lip curled slightly on the last word.

"You forgot Aunt Eliza," Joan said, tugging at her mother's sleeve.

"Hush! we're not supposed to talk about her," Nathan disapproved.

"Really, children! There is no need to give Miss Browning a bad impression of us," Lady Mair said. "My husband's aunt, Miss Eliza Falcon, lives on the estate in a small cottage. She's somewhat eccentric in her ways and I do not encourage Nathan and Joan to visit her. Now, if you wish to show Miss Browning to her room—I'll have Betsy bring you some hot water, Miss Browning. That coach much have been *very* dusty!"

She doesn't like me, Felice thought as she dropped a curtsey and followed the children out of the room. She thinks I am too young and too pretty.

"Father will be back next week," Nathan said. "He has been sitting in the House of Lords."

"He will bring us presents back," Joan said dreamily. "Father always brings presents back when he goes away, but he doesn't go away very often. He likes it best at home."

"It's a beautiful home," Felice said.

"We have four houses," Nathan explained. "There's the manor on the other side of the river and Wittle Farm over beyond the monastery ruins and Paget Place in Maidstone."

"And Witch's Dower," put in Joan.

"What a pretty name!" Felice exclaimed.

"That's Aunt Eliza's cottage. It belongs to her, not to Father." Nathan gave his sister a warning glance.

They were mounting the wide staircase. Below them the great hall stretched its length and towered above them to the hammerbeams of the roof; it brooded about them. The tapestries fluttered slightly as if the dim, embroidered figures longed to be free. Along the back wall of the gallery portraits were ranged, each in a gilt frame, and those too stared down hungrily, as if they envied the living.

"There have been Falcons here since fifteen hundred and thirty-six," Nathan said solemnly. "Both my parents are descended from the man who built *Kingsmead* because they are first cousins."

"I thought Lady Mair was Welsh," Felice commented.

"Her father was Welsh, but her mother was Apple Falcon and she was sister to my father's father," Nathan explained. "Great-Grandfather Edward had six children altogether. There was Prescott, who had my father, and Apple, who had my mother, and Nat, who was killed in battle, and Helen, who married and went away, and Weston, who still lives here—"

"And Aunt Eliza," said Joan, and again her brother flashed her the warning glance.

Felice paused, her eyes drawn toward the face of a young girl enclosed in one of the gilt frames. The face was beautiful, crowned with long red hair which flowed about slim shoulders. The girl in the frame had amber eyes that slanted like a cat's, and there was in her expression something infinitely sweet and infinitely yearning. The color of the hair was different, but the face was that of the green-clad creature she had seen fleetingly in the drive.

Joan's eyes followed the direction of her new governess's regard. "Isn't she pretty? That's Catrin Falcon," she volunteered. "Catrin was a—"

"Miss Browning doesn't want to hear you chattering your head off," Nathan interrupted hastily. His boyish face was crimson, and again he sent out the little warning glance.

Chapter 2

When Felice awoke the next morning she wondered
for a moment where she was, and then the memories
of the previous day rushed over her. She was a governess now.

Mindful of Lady Mair's scrutiny, she put on a shabby
brown dress which she tried to improve by threading
pink ribbon along the yoke. Certainly the dress made
her look more like a governess, and she stifled a sigh
as she twisted her unruly curls up into a chignon.

The house had proved both grander and more
homely than she had anticipated. Certainly the great
hall had struck awe in her, and all the apartments
were richly furnished, the drawing room in the west
wing being particularly fine. But the schoolroom above
it had been comfortable rather than ornate, and the
bedroom where she had slept was hung prettily and
simply in blue.

It was easy, despite its size, to find one's way about
Kingsmead, for the building was simple in design. Its
wings swept back to enclose a garden fragrant with
herbs. The two apartments over the solar and parlor

were those occupied by Lord and Lady Falcon; the
two rooms over the kitchens were for Felice and her
younger pupil. Nathan occupied a room at the
back of the house, and his great-uncle had the adjoin-
ing chamber.

Felice had met Weston briefly as the children had
shown her around. A plump, pink-faced old gentleman, he had emerged onto the gallery, bowed, smiled
vaguely, and wandered away again, a bunch of embroidery threads trailing from his fingers.

She ate her breakfast with the children in the schoolroom. No more was said about Aunt Eliza or about the
mysterious girl in the picture. Instead, the children
talked about their ponies and the way that John
spoiled their fun by refusing to allow them to gallop;
about their father, whom they obviously adored; about
Mr. Penn, who gave them sweets when they learned
their lessons well. Nathan and Joan were polite, lively children who had obviously been gently reared.
Teaching them, Felice decided, would be interesting.

Because it was Wednesday, the children were bound
for the parsonage for their instruction from the vicar.
Felice went down with them to the courtyard where a
pony trap stood waiting.

"Are you coming with us to meet Mr. Penn?" Nathan enquired.

"Oh, do come!" Joan begged, dancing from one foot
to the other.

Felice hesitated for a moment and then nodded.
After all, Lady Mair had told her that she might take
what exercise she chose when the children were occupied elsewhere. There was nothing to prevent her
from driving down into the village with them and ex-
ploring while they were with the vicar.

"If you take the reins, John will not have to come

with us," Nathan said. "Actually, I can manage them very well by myself, but Mama worries about us."

"Then why don't you take the reins now, while I watch you?" Felice suggested.

The boy's face brightened as he clambered up to the high seat and Joan, leaning out at a perilous angle, called gleefully to the groom who had just come around the side of the house, "We have no need of you this morning, John. Miss Browning will look after us." Felice had no way of knowing what John's reaction was, for Nathan slapped the reins over the pony's board back with a such joyful vigor that the trap jerked over the cobbles.

They were in the green tunnel again, up which she had walked the previous afternoon. An immense amount of time seemed to have elapsed between the two events. At the open gates Nathan swung the vehicle to the left with a dexterity that led Felice to realize he had been longing for an opportunity to show off his skill.

"It's three miles to the village," he said "The road dips to the right just before the bridge. One of my ancestors was killed there when the river broke its banks."

In the daylight she could see the hollow of Marie Regina tucked between river and meadows. Behind the tall spire of the church a graveyard spread itself to the limits of a low wall. On the other side of the road, a narrower path wound steeply into thick woods.

"The ruins of the old monastery are there," Nathan said, pointing to a hill beyond the river. It's slopes were wooded, and high on the hill broken fragments of stone were silhouetted against the blue skyline.

They drove down the winding street between the rows of neat houses with tiny gardens and white-

washed steps. At the end of the street a green patch
was crowded with stocks and benches and a maypole.
The sign from a timbered inn flapped in the warm
breeze. The parsonage was a neat square house beyond the church. As Felice went up the path, the
door opened and a thin gentleman in a cassock appeared on the threshold.

"Miss Browning? The children have been talking of
your impending arrival." His handshake was firm and
friendly.

"I thought I might explore a little while they are at
their lesson," Felice said.

"Most certainly, though I fear there's little of great
interest in the village apart from the actual buildings,
which are really quite ancient. Of course, if you have
antiquarian tastes, the ruins of the monastery are well
worth examination. The graveyard, too, contains some
rather interesting tombstones, if you are not inclined
to regard such things as morbid."

"Oh, I shall occupy myself," she assured him.

"We usually spend about two hours with Mr. Penn,"
Nathan informed her.

"Scripture this morning; on Fridays Nathan studies
Latin and Greek with me and Joan learns the secrets
of the culinary arts from my housekeeper," Mr. Penn
said.

"Then I'll call back at eleven." She consulted the
small watch pinned to her bodice.

"When there will be cakes and ale," the vicar promised, "or, to be more exact, hot chocolate and raspberry
tarts!"

Joan darted inside and her brother followed at a
more sedate pace. Mr. Penn gazed after them with the
same indulgent smile that their mother had worn.

"You will find them intelligent pupils," he said. "My

own mornings with them have always been very interesting, but then, the Falcons are a most interesting family, a most distinguished family, Miss Browning. At eleven, then?" He shook hands again and went inside.

Felice wandered down the path, lifting her face to the streaming sunshine. Halfway down a narrower strip of paving cut across the garden toward a lynch-gate. She made her way toward it and was soon in the churchyard, walking slowly between the headstones, some upright, others sunk deeper or tilted amid the green. Yew trees brooded over them and flowers sprang from the mounds of moss. She went up the sloping path that twisted round the church toward the graves beyond where the path ended, where stone and grass shared the land up to the low wall which marked the limits of the sacred enclosure.

A large tomb, much larger than the rest, drew her attention. It was big enough for several people to enter at once, but the door was secured by three padlocks. The figure of an angel bearing a sword brooded over the entrance.

It was, as she had expected, the Falcon tomb. The family names were inscribed in gold upon the door. She bent closer to read them, and was suddenly conscious of being watched. As she turned, her eyes caught a flash of green, and then the small girl she had seen in the drive the previous day stepped from behind a yew tree, staring at her. At such close range she was even more like the girl in the old portrait, save for her hair, which hung down over her shoulders but was a pale, silvery-gilt instead of red.

"Are you trying to find a way into the tomb?" the girl asked. Her voice was light and sweet, like the echo of a bell. Her eyes were a light greenish-grey, veiled by long lashes and down-tilted eyelids that gave her face a smooth, remote, mysterious aspect.

"I was looking for the names," Felice said.

"Because you are the new governess and wish to know about the children you are to teach, about their family? I can tell you about the Falcons," the girl said, raising her head proudly.

"Can you, indeed?" Felice smiled as she spoke, as if some part of her wished to humor the little elfish thing.

"There is a curse upon them," the girl said. "They didn't tell you that when they employed you, did they? But it's true; everybody knows it, though nobody talks about it."

"I don't believe in curses," Felice said.

"Then you wouldn't mind if somebody put one on you? Oh, I think you would! Anybody would. The Falcons do, though they'll not admit it. A witch put a curse on them long ago. Nobody knows why, except that a Falcon offended her once."

"What sort of curse?" Felice asked the question despite herself.

"Nobody knows that, either, but when a child with a crescent moon on her thigh is born into the family the words are given to her."

"Her?"

"The witch is always a woman," the girl said. "The words are passed down, you see."

"Superstition," Felice said, and smiled again.

"But they're an unlucky family," the girl told her. "Not the first Falcons who built the house before the witch came, but those who followed afterward."

"Who was it came?" Felice asked. She had no faith in such tales, but the girl's strange, secret amusement fascinated her.

"A Welshwoman. She wed her daughter to one of

the Falcons, but he was drowned one year when the river bust its banks. The villagers came to the daughter and found the witchmark on her, so they swam her in the river and she drowned, too. But it was the mother who had worked the evil, and she who passed down the words to the next one who bore the mark."

"And in what way was the family always unlucky?" Felice enquired.

"Look at the names," the girl pointed. "See the names."

"They are names, nothing more."

"And each one a Falcon, each one touched by the curse. There is the one who drowned." The girl read it out gleefully. "Sir Robert Falcon, born 1594, drowned 1617. He was the first one upon whom the curse fell. And lower down, see there, Charity Falcon—they say she was seduced by her husband's brother and died in giving birth to the child. And further down, Prayer Paget—she was born a Falcon on her mother's side, but she died when she was only ten years old. She was killed by a horse, they say, but there are others who think that her brother, Lord Charles, had something to do with it. They still tell tales of him in Marie Regina."

"There are always tales," Felice said.

"But not such as these," the girl said. "They say Charles Falcon never slept without a lighted candle by his bed, and that he was the one who ordered the tomb to be triple-locked so that the dead could not get at him. But he's there now. In the end he had to join them." She threw back her head and sent peal after peal of laughter echoing eerily up into the yew trees.

"Would you like to see where the witch girl is buried? she asked suddenly. "Not the one who laid the curse, for nobody knew at the time that she *was* a witch, but her daughter."

"The one who married the Falcon who was drowned in the flood?" Despite herself, Felice was interested.

The girl darted up the slope and vaulted the low wall as easily as a gazelle. Felice caught up her narrow skirt and followed, stumbling over the rough tussocks of grass. It took her a few minutes to scramble over the stones, and then she was at once ankle-deep in lush, sweet-scented grass.

The girl in green was standing a little distance away, her hands folded before her, her head bent. Her eyes were fixed upon a stone half-buried in the deep foliage.

Felice knelt and made out, with considerable difficulty, the inscription cut into the stone.

CATRIN FALCON
BORN 1594. DROWNED 1617

"They buried her outside the churchyard wall," the girl said. "She made no curse, you know, but they would not have her in sacred ground. Yet her mother Margred, who was truly evil, lies now in the Falcon tomb. Don't you think that is comic?"

"It's sad," Felice said. "I think it's very sad."

"Yes. You're right, of course." The beautiful face was still and serious. "It is extremely sad. Poor Catrin."

"Catrin?" Suddenly the name stabbed at Felice's memory. The girl in the portrait staring out of the frame—and Joan had said, "Isn't she pretty? That's Catrin Falcon." When Felice looked up again, the girl in the green dress was rapidly making her way across the field, her long, light hair floating about her shoulders, the grass springing up again after she trod it down.

Another figure, on horseback, was cantering toward Felice. As she rose to her feet, Lady Mair swung herself from the saddle. She looked handsome that morning in a severely tailored riding habit of leaf-green, with a small feathered hat on her head. She also looked extremely annoyed, though she obviously took pains to conceal it, saying with a faintly strained smile, "Miss Browning, I understand you dispensed with John's services and allowed Nathan to drive the trap into the village. I hope you are sufficiently expert yourself to qualify as instructor."

"I believe I am, Lady Mair," Felice spoke politely but her eyes met the other's steadily.

"And now you are taking some exercise. Did you meet Mr. Penn?"

"He was very cordial," Felice said.

"He's well-educated, a cut above most country clergymen." Lady Mair looped the reins of her mount over her arm and began to stroll alongside Felice. "I'm afraid there are few families of our standing in the neighborhood. However, neither my husband nor I are socially inclined. You were looking at the grave." The last few words were shot out rapidly.

"The girl in the green showed it to me," Felice explained.

"Had you wished to learn something of the family history, you could have applied to me for the information," the older woman said coldly. "The Falcons have lived at *Kingsmead* since the sixteenth century. It is perhaps not surprising that their history has, at times, been violent. Our ancestors, I'm told, were a lusty lot."

"But there was a witch?"

"A poor innocent girl who lost her husband through

a sad accident and was blamed by the villagers. She was tied up and swum by them. Had she been guilty, according to the superstition of the time, she would have floated. As it was, she proved her innocence by drowning, but they would not give her a churchyard burial for all that. Happily, we live in more enlightened times."

"And the curse?"

"Another foolish tale. The mother of the girl who was drowned is said to have put a curse on the family which is handed down throughout the generations. Fortunately, we live in a rational age when such stories are little heeded. I hope you will not discuss this with Nathan or Joan."

"No, of course not. It was the girl in green who spoke of it. She looked so much like the portrait—I mean, the portrait in the gallery, the one of Catrin—" Felice broke off uncomfortably, for Lady Mair's face had flamed scarlet, her lips thinning to a tight line.

"That girl has no connection to the family," she said icily.

"She seemed . . . strange, almost fey," Felice persisted.

"Willow Clegg is not in the least fey," the other said. "I must insist, Miss Browning, that you do not wander about gossiping with every village brat."

"No, of course not." Snubbed, Felice felt her own color mounting.

"Shall we walk down to the parsonage together and ask Mr. Penn to allow the children to break off early?" Lady Mair asked. She had regained her composure, and the glance she turned upon Felice was one of cool friendliness. They skirted the low wall and were again on the steep road leading to the village street. Several people nodded in friendly fashion as they went along, some of the men touching their forelocks, the women dropping brief curtseys.

"The general store contains most basic necessities," Lady Mair said. "For anything outside the general run of things we drive into Maidstone every month. There is a circulating library in Maidstone which you may care to join, though my husband's father amassed a considerably number of books. As we have no library proper, we keep them in the drawing room. You may borrow what you like."

They had reached the gate of the parsonage where Lady Mair handed Felice the reins of the horse and walked up the path without a backward glance.

"It looks," said Felice to herself ruefully, "as if I have just missed my cake and ale." The horse jerked its head and snorted as if in agreement.

It was fifteen minutes before the children made their appearance. They ran toward her, their faces beaming at the prospect of a holiday.

"Mama says she is going to ride home behind us and we are to have a picnic instead of dinner because the weather is so fine," Joan bubbled.

"May I unhitch the trap, Miss Browning?" Nathan asked eagerly. At Felice's nod the boy ran off with an air of importance to perform his task.

A few seconds later Lady Mair came out of the parsonage and strode toward them. She made no apology and offered no thanks as she took the reins from Felice and mounted. Yet her tone was pleasant enough as she said, "I have promised the children a picnic in the garden instead of dinner, but this afternoon you may have them all to yourself. You will want to know what level they have reached, and you must make a list of anything you need so that we may send into Maidstone for it. You will join us for the picnic, of course."

Her intention, if it was to put Felice at ease, failed. The girl blinked back lonely tears as she climbed up into the trap again. Every word had contrived to remind her that she was a stranger here—not an invited guest, but a paid servant. If she failed to please, she could be dismissed. And already she had made a bad beginning. Her blue dress had been too gay; she had asked too many questions; she had chattered about the family with a complete stranger. As if in obedience to her thought, the green-clad girl emerged from the trees at the other side of the main road and stood staring at them. This time she was not alone. At her side was a big golden retriever, its tail wagging, its ears pricked. As the trap passed the dog whined and strained at its leash as if in welcome.

"There's Willow and Beau," Joan said, twisting around in her seat.

"Hush! Mama is riding behind us," Nathan said. His hands tightened on the reins, the knuckles showing white.

"Willow is a sort of cousin," Joan began, and fell silent as her mother rode up beside them.

"You are handling the reins well," she said loudly to Nathan. "Keep them firm but not stretched. Your father will be pleased." If she had noticed the girl and the dog she said nothing, but her cheeks were scarlet again and she laid the whip across her own horse's neck with no gentle hand.

As they rumbled into the courtyard, Nathan let out a shout. "Father is come home! We didn't look for him till next week."

The tall figure hurried to the side of the trap, swinging Joan into his arms. Over her head his blue eyes met Felice's, and he showed blunt white teeth in a smile.

"Miss Browning, if I had known my business in London would end so quickly, I would have asked you to wait for an extra day so that we could have had the pleasure of travelling here together," he said. "I hope my children have not run you ragged!"

"We haven't had any lessons yet," Nathan said. "We went down to see Mr. Penn as usual this morning, but Mama said we were to come home early—"

"Because there's going to be a picnic!" Joan shrieked.

"Am I invited?" her father enquired, setting her on her feet and handing Felice down.

"Of course you're invited, Father," Nathan said. "And Miss Browning is coming, too."

"But not in that somber gown, surely." His blue eyes flicked over the shabby brown stuff with its trimming of cheap ribbon. "You were wearing a much prettier dress when I saw you in London—blue or some such shade."

"It seemed a little frivolous for a governess," she stammered.

"Nonsense! Governesses ought to encourage learning by making themselves as pretty as possible," he said heartily. "Mair! Mair, my love, do persuade Miss Browning to put off this dismal color. I'm sure you'll agree that she ought to wear a prettier shade."

Felice had not noticed Lady Mair, who stood by her horse and smiled, color still blazing in her cheeks and her brown eyes cold as stones.

"Miss Browning looks charming in blue," Lady Mair said graciously, if somewhat stiffly. "It brings out the color of her eyes."

"Then Miss Browning shall run upstairs and change her gown," Lord Falcon said. "Nathan, you handled those reins remarkably well. And Joan, you minx, I believe you've grown a foot since I was home. Don't you think so, Mair?"

As Felice went into the great hall she could feel, rather than see, the cold brown eyes following her.

Chapter 3

It was a week before Felice was at liberty again, for the children occupied most of her attention, and when she went out of the schoolroom Lady Mair was always there with linen to be mended or lace to be darned. She saw very little of Lord Falcon, who rose early and spent most of the day out-of-doors, and on the rare occasions they did run across each other, either Nathan or Joan was there, too.

Teaching was both easier and harder than she had expected. The children were bright, so bright that she often had her work cut out to keep ahead of them, but Nathan, despite his sweet temper, had an obstinate streak, and Joan was a chatterbox. It was difficult to induce her to sit still and concentrate, for her attention was constantly straying to the window, or to the dolls sitting in a neat row along the shelf, or to the musical box with the little dancer on top who pirouetted when the key was turned.

"It's more than a hundred years old," Joan had said importantly. "It belonged to a little girl called Prayer who died when she was only ten. She was killed by a

37

horse, you know. Don't you think Prayer is a strange
name for a little girl, Miss Browning?"

Prayer was the child the green-clad girl had mentioned, the one whose brother would not sleep in the
dark. Felice had not seen the blonde girl again. Though
she dutifully attended church on Sunday with the
family, she saw no sign of the girl, and she was reluctant to reveal her curiosity to her pupils.

It was not until the following Wednesday when
the children went down to the parsonage that Felice
had the opportunity of going for a walk. The sun
was shining, and a week's confinement to the house
had made Felice restless. As soon as Lady Mair had
ridden through the arch, Felice reached out for her
bonnet and shawl and went lightly down the stairs.

Instead of taking the long drive which wound to the
main road she turned to the left, skirting the courtyard
wall and coming out into the open fields which sloped
toward the wooded banks of the river.

It was pleasant to walk with no one tugging at her
sleeve to ask her questions; to go at her own pace with
no thoughts of the mending waiting for her nimble
fingers. The countryside was beautiful, and the shadow which seemed to hang over the great house was
lifted for a spell. She was among the trees, and the
sunlight was broken up into dazzling particles of gold
making patterns on the moss-clad ground. Ahead she
could hear the gurgling of the river. Nathan had explained to her, "The land on the other side of the river
used to belong to the Fleets, but my great-grandfather
married Joanna Fleet and so all the land became part
of the Falcon estate." "The old manor is still there,"
Joan had put in. "It's all locked up now, but there's
furniture in it and curtains at the windows. Mama
says the place ought to be rented out, but Father won't

have it." "We're not supposed to know about that," Nathan had interrupted. To Felice he had said apologetically, "She sometimes listens to private conversations."

Felice had smiled and drawn their attention back to the map they were tracing. Joan's comment had been one more small puzzle to file away in her mind: the girl called Willow Clegg who looked so much like the witch-girl; the aunt who lived in the estate cottage but was never mentioned; the furnished manor house where nobody lived. Beneath the tranquil, domestic atmosphere of *Kingsmead* flowed strange currents.

A shrill, excited barking stopped her in her tracks. Deep in thought, she had failed to notice that the trees were thinning out into a glade, and that ahead of her a small white house blocked her way. It was a pretty place, creeper-covered and gleaming with paint, with bramble bushes and apple trees and lavender mixed up together all about it, and a lean-to stable built on at one end.

The golden dog was still barking, its feet planted firmly in her path.

"Beau! Hush your noise, boy!" The voice, crisp and loud, issued from the open door of the cottage and was followed by the emergence of a tall, grey-haired woman in breeches and boots with a frying pan in her hand and a mobcap perched on top of her head.

"No need to be afraid of Beau," the woman said cheerfully. "He's an old dog, for all he looks so spry, but he never bit anyone even when he was young. You're Felice Browning, I take it."

"And you're Miss Eliza Falcon." Felice held out her hand shyly to have it warmly shaken in a brisk, no-nonsense fashion.

"Come and have some mead," the older woman invited, "and call me Aunt Eliza. Everybody else in the village does."

The front door opened into a long, low room out of which narrow stairs twisted. Through another door at the foot of the stairs Felice could see a second apartment lined with cupboards and shelves.

"Come and sit by the fire," Aunt Eliza said. "We don't need one really, but the apple wood smells so sweet."

"Thank you." Seating herself in one of the two high-backed chairs, Felice looked round with interest. The room was a curious mixture of the old and the new, the expensive and the shoddy. Braided rugs in vivid shades covered the floor, a silver clock inlaid with mother-of-pearl ticked away the hours, a crystal vase held a motley assortment of weeds and grasses. The mug which Eliza handed to her was decorated with gold leaf and chipped.

"Drink up. I brewed it myself," Eliza said. She had put down the frying pan and, pouring herself a generous measure, sat down opposite, her elbows on her knees.

"So you're the new governess. James said you were very pretty," she remarked.

"Lord Falcon comes here?"

"When he can get away from the Welsh termagent he married. I'll wager she's already giving you a difficult time. The trouble with Mair is she cannot forget that James was once in love with somebody else before he met her. Every pretty female is suspect in her eyes. You don't think it well-bred in me to talk about my nephew's wife, eh?"

"I'm sure I don't know," Felice said helplessly.

"Willow told me she'd been talking to you," Aunt Eliza said.

"Willow . . . Clegg?" Felice looked at her with interest.

"She lives with me. Didn't she tell you?"

"She only told me about the witch-girl," Felice said. "The one called Catrin whose mother put a curse on the—" She broke off uncomfortably, but Eliza laughed.

"No need to get in a taking because I'm a Falcon," she said comfortably. "It's years since I set foot in the big house."

"Oh?" Above the rim of the mug Felice's blue eyes were wide with curiosity.

"It goes back to when I was a girl," Eliza said. "There were six of us in the family then. My eldest brother, Prescott, was the father of twin boys, Fairfax and James. James is the present Lord Falcon. Prescott and his wife were killed in a carriage accident when the twins were quite small. My own mother . . . she died before the boys were born. She killed herself. To understand why, you'd have had to know my father, Edward Falcon. He was an evil, possessive man, Miss Browning. A man to whom land and money meant everything and people nothing. Only Prescott was allowed to marry, for it was his duty to sire an heir for the estate. My young brother, Nat, died unwed, and Weston—you'll have met Weston?"

"Yes, but he stays in his room most of the time."

"To avoid Mair, if you ask me. Mind, one cannot blame her for being sharp with him. He's a weak, silly powderpuff of a man, is Weston." Eliza sighed and took a swig of the mead.

"You had sisters," Felice prompted.

"Helen and Apple," Eliza nodded. "Apple's real name was Abigail. My sisters both wed—defied my father and wed. Helen was middle-aged, but she went away and we never heard from her again. Apple married an artist, a Welshman, when she was practically still a child, and we heard nothing of her for nearly thirty years."

"But you didn't wed?"

"Never felt the lack of a mate," Eliza said. "From what I saw of my parent's marriage, a woman's wisest to remain a maid, unless she craves children. After Prescott and his wife were killed, I had the twin boys to rear, and then Willow. I've enjoyed the best of life, I think." She raised her head proudly, and Felice felt her soul move with compassion and admiration for this triumphant old woman who was so unlike herself.

"Fairfax was the elder twin, the one expected to inherit the peerage and all the land," Eliza continued. "He was a handsome lad, but restless. James was always the steady one, with a love of the land deep in his heart."

"And Willow Clegg?"

"Her mother was Huldah Clegg. Huldah's father was the bailiff at Wittle Farm—that's another of the Falcon properties, on the other side of the hill past the ruins. Willow was Huldah's daughter, Huldah's and Fairfax's."

"The elder twin wed the bailiff's daughter?" Felice asked in surprise.

"They were never wed," Eliza replied briskly. "Fairfax seduced and deserted her. He went off to fight with Lord Nelson, and when Huldah had borne her child she followed him. Dressed herself as a lad and served in the Navy, did Huldah. She and Fairfax were both killed at Trafalgar." Her high-colored face was sad for a moment, mourning the passing of something young and fair.

"And the child . . . you reared her?"

"My father would not acknowledge that the babe

had any claim upon the family," Eliza said. "This cottage belongs to me; it's not part of the main estate, so I left *Kingsmead* and brought the babe here. She's thirteen years old."

"And Lady Mair won't accept her? Surely that's unjust," Felice exclaimed.

"Ah, she has reason for it in her own mind," Eliza said tolerantly. "You see, James did love somebody else before he married her. It was Huldah Clegg he loved. He even fixed the old manor house up as a home for them both. But she listened to Fairfax with his silver tongue, and the manor house has stayed empty ever since."

"And Lady Mair?"

"She is Apple's child," Aunt Eliza said. "We never even knew she existed until she came here with word of her parents' deaths. My father would have turned her out, too, but Mair is strong-willed. James fell in love with her and wed her, but she's never accepted the fact that he loved somebody else first. And so I am not welcome back at my old home, and Willow is not accepted as a member of the family, save by James. He has a fondness for us both, and so he comes to see us and takes an interest in Willow."

"It's very kind of you to tell me all this," Felice said.

"And you're wondering why I have told you." The blue eyes were shrewd. "Well, it's not a tale I'd pour into just any ear, but since you're here at *Kingsmead*, teaching my great-nephew and great-niece, you might as well have the true story and not a lot of half-truths and crazy superstitions."

"You don't believe in the curse, then?" Felice enquired.

Eliza set down her mug and rose, frowning into the fire. "There was a curse," she said slowly. "I don't know the words of it, nor why it was spoken in the first place, but there was a curse. The one who cursed our family also planted the tree which grows outside the courtyard. And it's true that from time to time a woman is born into our family with the mark of a crescent moon on her thigh. She who bears the mark is given the words of the curse. I know that's true, for my sister Apple carried the mark and learnt the curse from an old aunt of ours. But the words died with Apple, I suppose, and there is nobody to tell Willow."

"Why should she know them?"

"Willow also has the crescent moon on her thigh," Eliza said reluctantly. "She heard talk of the curse from some of the village folk when she was little and wouldn't rest until she had wormed the rest of the story out of me—everything save the actual words. They died with Apple." She broke off, listening as the deep-throated bark sounded again from outside.

"It's James," she said, moving swiftly to the door. "James has ridden down to see me."

He bent his head under the lintel, hugged Aunt Eliza and smiled across at Felice. His teeth were white in his brown face and his fair hair was tipped white. "Miss Browning, so you and Aunt Eliza have found each other," he said cordially.

"I hope it was in order to come here," Felice began nervously.

"I'm glad that you did," he said. "My aunt has too few visitors."

"I choose my friends," Eliza said. "Miss Browning is a very charming young lady, James."

"The children are fond of her already," he told her. "It will brighten us up to have a new face around the estate, and a pretty one, too! Don't you think Miss Browning is pretty?"

"Exceedingly pretty," his aunt said drily. "I did wonder if you'd noticed. Will you have a drink?"

"I'm on my way home," he said. "I came to see Willow. I have something for her."

"A gift? Oh, she'll be so pleased."

"Come and see," he invited. "You, too, Miss Browning."

The gift stood in the middle of the clearing, its ears pricked, its nostrils twitching, its creamy sides burnished.

"A pony? James, this looks like a valuable animal," Eliza said.

"Willow ought to have a mount of her own," James said. "Nathan and Joan have the pick of the stables between them, and Willow is a Falcon, too. I don't know if Miss Browning—"

"I've made Willow's position clear to her," Eliza said.

"Is Willow here?" He looked around.

"She's been out since dawn. Beau wanted to go with her, but his legs aren't what they used to be, are they, boy?" Eliza bent to stroke his gleaming coat.

"Did you walk all the way over from *Kingsmead?*" James asked Felice.

"I was walking in the woods. I came upon the cottage by accident," Felice said quickly. She did not want him to think that she had run down to gossip with his aunt as soon as Lady Mair was out.

"I must find a good saddlehorse for your use," he said. "Aunt Eliza, tell Willow the pony's name is Silver. I'll be down again next week. Do you have everything you need? You mentioned last time I saw you that your stock of wheat flour was low."

"I have everything I need, and more," she assured him, patting his shoulder.

"Then I'll take Miss Browning back, to be in time for

dinner." He turned and lifted her to the saddle of his own horse as easily as if she were a child, kissed his aunt on the cheek and tweaked the bow on her mob-cap, and led his horse out of the clearing into the dappled trees.

Over his shoulder he said, "You must think ours a strange family, Miss Browning. I hope what my aunt told you won't change your mind about staying with us?"

"No, of course not," she said, coloring with embarrassment.

"Mair is—she finds it very difficult to accept Willow as a member of the family," he said. "And as my aunt will not go where Willow is not invited, she never comes to *Kingsmead*. Does that make me sound as if I am not master in my own house?"

Felice crimsoned even more, for that very thought had flashed across her mind.

"Did my aunt tell you—did she tell you that I had hoped to marry Willow's mother once?" he asked. "I was too dull for her, I fear. My brother was more exciting, more . . . I never blamed her. I never blamed either of them. Least of all do I blame that poor child. But Mair, she finds that difficult to understand. Women like to be the first love in a man's life, Miss Browning."

"I would like to be a man's last love," Felice said shyly.

"A young lady as pretty as you are should have no difficulty in becoming just that for some fortunate gentleman," he said, smiling up at her.

"A penniless governess," she said wryly.

"When you find a young gentleman," he promised, "I'll make certain you have a dowry."

"Oh, but I couldn't!" she exclaimed.

"You are one of my responsibilities now," James said firmly, "and it would be my pleasure to see you comfortably settled. Not too soon, mind, for I would like my children to have the benefit of your instruction for a year or two. But when you find a young gentleman, it will be my privilege to give you away and to ensure that you do not go empty-handed to your bridegroom. Come! You have my pledge upon it." He had paused and stretched out his hand, laying it over her own, smiling up at her.

Among the trees something flashed briefly green and was gone before either of them noticed. Willow Clegg ran swiftly, her bare feet moving unerringly between the roots and clumps of creeper that grew in the darker parts of the wood. Her thin hand was clapped across her mouth, but the eyes above glinted with malicious laughter.

So Uncle James and that silly, namby-pamby governess are in love! she thought. They rode down in the woods together, whispering, holding hands, and she has not been here above a week!

Willow had been out since dawn. Staying indoors irritated her, for she disliked the confinement of walls and roof and was happiest out in the green fields or the solitude of the woods. Most of all she liked to be down by the river, watching the darting fish, plunging her hands into the icy water and feeling the shock of it through her nerves, as if the blood in her own veins had cooled like the blood of the sea-creatures.

The other children in the village disliked her. She had seen the older women make the sign against the evil eye when she passed. There had been a time when these things had hurt her, but that time was past, for she had discovered that if she wished very hard, with her whole soul, the people who offended her generally met with misfortune. There had been a boy in the village who had thrown stones at her. She had run away crying, but as the tears dried she had begun to build up a picture in her mind. She had imagined him lying very still and white with his leg twisted beneath him, and the very next day Aunt Eliza had told her that the boy had fallen and broken his leg. It had pleased Willow to hear that, it had given her a sense of triumph. She was no longer Willow Clegg, whom nobody wanted, but a person of importance, who held in her mind a great power.

She used the spell only rarely, fearing that it might weaken if she used it too often on people who did not matter. If only she knew the actual words of that ancient curse, she would be able to do anything she pleased.

"But my sister Apple never told anybody," Aunt Eliza had said. "The words died with her, and it's best that they should. There is too much unhappiness in the world, child, for us to pass it down from one generation to the next."

Aunt Eliza, Willow thought scornfully, is a fool. She should have made her sister repeat the words. Now there was nobody to give those words to Willow, who surely had a right to them, bearing as she did the mark of a crescent moon upon her thigh.

Uncle James she also regarded as a fool, for instead of taking Aunt Eliza and herself back to live at *Kingsmead*, he gave in meekly to his wife. The fact that he visited the cottage frequently and brought them gifts counted for nothing in Willow's eyes. What she did notice and remember was that she been taught how to read and write by Aunt Eliza, but that a fancy governess had been engaged for Nathan and Joan.

She was hiding under the bridge near the shallows

of the river when she saw Uncle James leading a strange pony toward the cottage. She guessed at once that it was for her, and part of her wanted to run up to him and fling her arms about his neck to thank him. Then she remembered that Joan had had a pony of her own since her third birthday, and the impulse died.

And now she had seen Uncle James with Miss Browning. That knowledge was another secret to hold close within herself, and perhaps to use in time to come.

If there was one person in the world whom Willow hated, it was Lady Mair. Her uncle's wife had never made any secret of her contempt for the girl or for Eliza. She never visited the cottage, and when she passed Willow in the village or on the road she looked down her nose, as if she caught a bad smell. It was splendid to have a secret which would hurt Lady Mair.

Felice, clinging to the pommel of the high saddle, watched the back of Lord Falcon's head as he led the horse across the sloping meadows toward the ivied walls of *Kingsmead*. This man, she knew instinctively, was one of those rare beings who are good and kind to the finest fibers of their natures. This was a man who would always do what he believed to be right, a man who would try not to cause any pain to those he loved.

"I wish," she thought, with the tug of loneliness at her heart, "that I was among those whom he loved."

As Felice was lifted to the ground she was aware of the strength of her employer's arms, the blueness of his eyes. The temptation to raise her hand and touch his cheek was so overwhelming that she muttered her thanks incoherently and hurried indoors with her head bent.

She was making her way along the gallery when the sensation of being watched came over her so strongly that she swung about. Her frightened, guilty eyes met the painted eyes of the witch-girl—clear, sweet eyes, with something in them that might have been a warning.

Chapter 4

"The gypsies are back," Mair said, drawing her lips down in displeasure.

"They come every year," James said comfortably, pouring himself another cup of coffee.

"They are a menace to the neighborhood," she said.

"Oh, come! you exaggerate, surely," he protested mildly. "The Romanies have been coming into Kent for centuries."

"They're thieves and vagabonds."

"Hard-working folk who choose to live differently from the way we live. The add color to the landscape."

"You are too easy with them," Mair frowned.

"Would you have me set about them with my riding crop?" he asked, amused. "I am not that type of person, my love."

"I know." She sighed as she spoke, because his gentleness exasperated her, and yet because she loved him she would not have him any different.

"They will do no harm," he promised. "I'll have a

51

word with old Sarah. She keeps that entire tribe in order."

"A filthy old crone who puffs on a clay pipe," Mair said crossly.

"She admires *you*," James said wryly. "Told me last year that my wife was a fine woman, almost good enough to be a gypsy."

"She had better keep her opinions to herself," Mair snapped. Her own brown complexion was a source of secret misery to her. It had not seemed to matter when she was a girl, living on the small Welsh farm where she was born. But when her parents had died and she had travelled into Kent and fallen in love with her cousin, she had longed passionately for white skin and yellow hair. They said that Huldah Clegg was a blonde, blue-eyed girl . . . Every time Mair looked at Willow she saw the girl who had borne a child to James's brother and died with that brother on the deck of a ship at Trafalgar.

"I will tell Nathan and Joan that they must stay close to the house," she said. "One hears of children being stolen—"

"By the gypsies? They can make enough babes of their own."

"Not rich babes who will inherit title and land," she argued.

James, who detested arguments, drank the dregs of his coffee in silence. Mair has been in a bad humor recently, he thought. Perhaps she is tired. Yet he knew there was little to make her tired since Miss Browning now took charge of the two children for most of the day.

"Perhaps you would like to go away for a little while," he suggested.

"Away? Where would we go?" she asked in surprise.

"We could go to London for a few days," he said.

"In the middle of haymaking?" she asked in disbelief. "When you only returned from the city last month?"

"If you truly feel discontented—" he began.

"I never said I was discontented," she interrupted.

"A little restless, then. I could spare a few days, my dear."

"You would hate it," she said. "You are never happy away from *Kingsmead*. You know you are not; and I would not be happy away from you."

"Shall we give a dinner party?" he suggested.

"There is nobody worth inviting," Mair objected.

"And you have nothing to wear. All ladies tell the same tale."

"I have too many dresses and no occasions at which to wear them."

"But, my love, I have just offered to give a dinner party."

"I don't want a dinner party," Mair said loudly.

"Then we won't have one," he said patiently.

She gave an exasperated shrug and rose from her place, her long skirts rustling indignantly. The delicate pastel muslins and high turbans of the period suited her little, and she had had the wisdom to retain a style of dressing which enhanced her tall figure and thin features. Her robes of dark red and green and bronze flattered her brown eyes and dark chestnut hair. Yet she never looked in a mirror without a little sinking in her heart.

James, watching her, tried to think of something that would please her. He loved his wife deeply; he even enjoyed her outbursts of temper. If he wished sometimes for more gentleness and understanding where Aunt Eliza and Willow were concerned, he reminded himself that Mair was a strong-principled woman who intended to rear her children with no stain of scandal on them.

Casting about for something to please his wife, James said, "Don't you feel that it would be more convenient if we were all to sit together to supper?"

"*All?*" Mair paused and stared at him with raised eyebrows.

"The children and Miss Browning, I mean. Nathan is quite old enough to sit to table in the evening, and Joan is not a baby. It would save the maids having to serve two meals as well."

He was right, of course. In justice she had to admit that, but supper was the only meal when she had him entirely to herself. At breakfast he seldom snatched more than a bite before riding out, and at dinner the children were there with their governess. This last meal of the day, when they sat together at the end of the long table, was their private time. She had always cherished it.

"It must be very dull for Miss Browning," James pursued the subject tactlessly.

"Dull? Has she been complaining of dullness?"

"No, of course not. She's a very sweet-natured young girl, but she *is* young. The company of children cannot be very exciting for her."

"If she is as young as all that, I'd have imagined that their company suited her ideally," Mair snapped. "Or is it that *you* are bored with *my* company?"

Color high in her cheeks, her eyes sparkling with temper, she looked at that moment extremely handsome. James smiled at her indulgently, his own temper unruffled. "I could never be bored with your company, my love," he said equably. "We won't alter the present arrangements if you don't wish."

"Oh, by all means, let us sit down to supper together," she said loudly. "Why not have the servants to sit down with us, too?"

"That was the custom in the old days," he said. "A pleasant custom, I think. I've often wished we could revive it."

Mair glanced at him, her mind searching for words to jolt him out of his complacency, but the tapping of feet on the stone stairs interrupted the argument.

"Come and join us, Miss Browning," James invited. "Will you have some coffee?"

"Oh, no, thank you. I wondered if I might go out for a little while?" Felice asked.

"At this hour? It's past eight?" Mair frowned at the clock instead of Felice.

"It's still light," Felice said. "I won't be more than an hour or two."

"But to leave the children and go out in the evening—"

"Nathan is reading and Joan is already asleep," Felice said quickly. "I want to go to church, if I may."

"To church in the middle of the week?" Mair looked amused.

"It's the anniversary of my parents' marriage," Felice explained. "We . . . we always went to church on that day to say a prayer together."

"And you wish to go tonight? To your own church, I suppose?" James gave her a sympathetic glance.

"I had not thought you so devout," Mair said lightly.

"It was a tradition," Felice said simply.

"And tradition is important," James said.

"Surely the priest won't be there," Mair said.

"No, but the church is open. I could go in, just for

a few minutes." She twisted her hands together nervously under her cloak, wishing that Lady Mair would not look at her in that cold, considering way.

"Certainly she must go," James said heartily. "I will ride with you, Miss Browning."

"Oh, but that's not necessary," Felice protested.

"Certainly it is not," Mair agreed promptly. "Miss Browning knows her way to her own church, and it is very light, as she says."

"A young lady ought to have an escort," James began.

"John can go with her. You have been out all day already," Mair said.

"If I might be allowed to go," Felice said, a little desperately.

"Ask John to escort you," Mair said, "though I cannot promise he will be very willing to go. He has already been over to Maidstone once today."

Felice curtsied and went out, conscious of her employers' regard as she tugged open the heavy door.

"Perhaps I ought to have insisted—" James began.

"Oh, do stop fussing," Mair said wearily. "Miss Browning will be perfectly all right. Shall we go into the solar?"

"If you wish, my love." James rose from his seat. "I'll go upstairs and ask Nathan to join us." He was already mounting the stairs. Their time together was spoiled, for much as she loved Nathan she resented sharing James with anybody, even their own son. Desire swept through her like hunger and she closed her eyes, wishing that he would run back down the stairs and hold her tightly, but he continued up the stairs, and she heard his voice raised cheerfully, "Nathan are you coming down to sit with us? Ask Uncle Weston to come down, too. He must not spend every evening in his room."

Felice saddled the mare that had been set aside for her use and rode away from *Kingsmead* alone. She had not missed the implication of Lady Mair's last words. Obviously, she was becoming a nuisance in the older woman's eyes, and there was always the danger that her value as a governess would count for nothing if Lady Mair decided she was becoming too much of a burden. "I would be very sorry to lose such a good position," she told the horse. "I would be very sorry to leave Nathan and Joan." It would be even harder to leave Lord Falcon, but to admit that even to herself was beyond her powers.

She rose across the meadows toward the deer park, beyond which the open common stretched. There were caravans strung across the grass, and the sound of quarrelling children echoed faintly. The sun was still warm, though the blue shadows were lengthening, and the tree-shaded park which bounded the edge of *Kingsmead* showed pools of gloom where the moss was already black-velvet.

The tiny church where mass was offered once a month was at the other side of the common. It was no more than a makeshift building designed to accommodate the small number of Catholics who lived in the outlying districts, but there was a pristine freshness about its white-painted altar and rows of cane-seated chairs. It was restful to sit there, easier in such a place to remember her parents and the life they had made together, easier, too, to separate herself for a while from thoughts of the Falcons, from longing for that which was not hers.

The path narrowed, branches of elm and alder lacing together above her head. Felice caught a gleam of white as some stray rabbit dashed behind a tree, and then a muffled thud made the earth quiver; someone trod cautiously behind the thicket.

She dismounted and parted the creepers. Her first thought was that Willow Clegg had followed her and was spying upon her, but the figure that stared back at her was that of a hulking, thick-set man with the bloodied carcass of a rabbit hanging from his fingers. His eyes, narrowed under a thatch of greying hair, focused upon her sharply.

"You're trespassing," Felice said loudly to cover her fear and nervousness. "This is Falcon land."

"Be it so?" His voice and eyes mocked her.

"Lord Falcon will be very angry when he hears. Poaching is a serious offense."

"And you'll be the one to tell him, eh?" He dropped the rabbit and began to move toward her, his shoulders hunched, his head thrust forward.

"I live at *Kingsmead*," she said above the beating of her heart. "Lord Falcon employs me as a governess for his children."

"Governess? And be you willing to teach me my letters, little lady?"

There was something different about his expression now; something furtive and lip-licking. His hands were reaching out toward her. He was so close that she could smell the ale on his breath.

As she turned to seize her horse's bridle, his hand jerked her back and the thin stuff of her gown ripped. "I will tell Lord Falcon," she began in a high, trembling voice, but the man laughed and his voice rumbled in her ears like the threat of thunder.

"You'll tell nobody, little lady. You'll tell nobody at all."

Worse than the voice and the eyes and the clutching

hands was his chuckle as she fought him, her throat closing upon a scream, her heels slipping on the moss. Nearby the dead rabbit began to stiffen.

At *Kingsmead* Lady Mair sat with a piece of embroidery in her hands and made an occasional half-hearted jab with the needle. She would have liked to fling everything away and invite James to retire for the night, but he was immersed in some news-sheet or other. He had not spoken in an age, and when he did she jumped slightly and pricked her finger.

"Don't you think so, my dear?"

"Don't I think what?" She sucked her finger and glared at him.

"Don't you think Miss Browning ought to be back by now? It's quite dark."

"Didn't John go with her?"

"I don't think so. I heard him down in the yard a little while ago, while I was looking in on Joan."

"You fuss too much," she told him, more out of a desire to argue than any real conviction. "Joan never wakes at night, and if she does it is Miss Browning's task to see to her."

"Except that she is not yet home," he frowned. "It is not wise for a young lady to ride alone across the common—"

"Because of the gypsies? You're the one who swears that they're harmless."

"Perhaps I ought to step out and see." He had put the paper aside and was rising to his feet.

I want you to stay here with me, her mind cried. I want you to forget that you have other folk in your care. I want you to look only at me, think only of me. "Do as you please," she said sourly, and began to sew with great concentration. "It's my belief she's quite able to fend for herself, but you can send John to look for her, though he'll not thank you. The servants have plenty of work to keep them occupied without dragging them out in their leisure time."

"There's somebody at the door." As the heavy knocker rose and fell, James hurried to open it, his face anxious.

Mair, from her place by the fire, heard a muffled exclamation, and then a sallow-faced young man entered, bearing in his arms an unconscious Felice. Her husband, his own face drained of color, exclaimed, "My dear, the most terrible thing seems to have happened. This gentleman—"

"Evans. Guto Evans." The man gave a brief nod.

"She has been attacked," James said, his voice quiet with horror. "She has been attacked, my dear."

Felice moaned suddenly and began to writhe. Her eyes, opening slowly, were blank with shock, her dark curls matted with twigs and leaves.

"I'll take her upstairs," James said. "Let me have her, sir. She will be frightened if she sees a stranger."

The man relinquished his burden readily enough, saying, "I am a medical man, sir. Dr. Guto Evans. I was on my way to visit my grandmother's people."

"Evans? In Marie Regina?"

"My grandmother was pure Romany, sir. Her youngest son married out of the tribe, a Welsh girl. They saved up enough to send me to university and medical school."

"May we hear your history later?" James interrupted, in a rare showing of irritation. "Mair, get the brandy and some hot water. She will need tending."

"I'll come up at once." She answered serenely, but her cheeks burned with temper. He was giving her orders as if she were a servant, as if the only thing in the world that mattered was the limp figure cradled in his arms. Hurrying into the kitchen to rouse the maids, Mair thought with deep and growing resentment, How typical of the silly creature to allow herself to be attacked. And how clever of her to know that compassion is my dear husband's besetting weakness. Felice moaned and clutched at James as if she suspected him of dropping her.

"I'll be there now," Mair called. "Dr. Evans, will you have the goodness to go upstairs, too? I'm sure your skill will be needed." And she will not be left alone to cling to my husband, to waken that dangerous compassion in his nature that dilutes the passion he has for me. Her mouth set, her eyes lowered, she applied herself to her task.

"This is a shocking occurrence," James said. Half an hour had passed and the three of them were in the hall again, the two gentlemen with glasses of rum in their hands, Mair seated between them with her fingers tensely entwined. Felice had dropped into a deep slumber, her face white against the pillow, her lashes dark crescents. She looked young and bruised, and the older woman was ashamed of her own jealous pain.

"A poacher, was all she could say of him," James said. "A dark-skinned poacher. I am reluctant to admit it, but it does seem that—" He paused and shot an uncomfortable glance toward the young doctor.

"A gypsy! I told you that it was foolish of you to allow them to camp here summer after summer. I told you—"

"I'll ride into Maidstone and swear a warrant," James said.

"If he came from the tribe he will be punished by them," Dr. Evans said. "I know my father's people. They settle these matters in their own way, and by morning they'll be gone."

"The man should be punished according to law—" James began

"But you cannot expect Miss Browning to give evidence in court on such a matter," Mair exclaimed. "It would be too much of an ordeal for any young woman, James."

"You're perfectly right." James looked contrite. "Miss Browning is gently bred. When I think of that brute with his hands on her—I feel like taking a shotgun and seeking him out myself."

"It would serve our purpose better if I were to go back to the camp and make some enquiries. They will talk more freely to a *poshrat*."

"A *poshrat?*" Mair's lips curled slightly.

"A part-gypsy. I am not ashamed of my origins."

"Not should you be." James spoke with the slightly embarrassed heartiness of a man who believes himself in the presence of a social inferior. "We are most grateful to you for finding Miss Browning and bringing her home."

"It was sheer chance," the doctor said. "Had I not decided to take a short-cut through the woods back to the village—I didn't realize I was trespassing."

"Are you staying in Marie Regina?" Mair asked politely.

"I am hoping to set up a practice here," the doctor explained. "I've been working at Guy's these past four years, gaining experience in new surgical techniques, but this part of the world has always attracted me."

"We already have a physician," James said.

"An old man who has more notion of how to treat horses than people," Mair said quickly. "A younger man would be most welcome." She smiled at Evans graciously.

"Your ladyship is very kind." He afforded her a

slight bow, his eyes scarcely concealing his admiration of her handsome figure and high color.

"And Miss Browning—she will suffer no lasting damage?" James brought them back to the events of the evening.

"She has had a terrible experience," Dr. Evans said, with a tinge of reproof in his voice. "But she is young and healthy and the mind can quickly learn to forget. Of course, if there is a child—"

"A child! Is it possible?"

"Very possible, milord, after such an event as rape." Dr. Evans spoke wryly.

"Poor Miss Browning! Poor little girl!" James's face was tight with distress. Watching him, Mair felt her own generous inclination to pity drain away. She said harshly, "We could never countenance such a thing! Miss Browning will have to leave."

"Leave? My dear, have you taken leave of your senses?" James asked. "We could not possible turn the poor child away for something that was not her fault. If I had ridden over with her to the church this evening—I shall always blame myself most bitterly."

"If you will excuse me." The doctor put down his glass and rose. "I will go back to the camp and see if I can discover anything. I will come by tomorrow morning to check upon Miss Browning and to give you the information I have gleaned. It's my opinion that a private justice will have been meted out already, if the matter is known. Rapists often boast, you know."

"I am not acquainted with many rapists," Mair said archly. Her brown eyes twinkled as she offered Dr. Evans her hand. If she allowed herself to glance at James she would explode into fury, for he was gazing at the stairs as if the smallest sound from above would cause him to leap up them.

"I will call tomorrow," Evans said again.

When she came back to the fire, James was still gazing up the stairs. "I blame myself," he said briefly. "I ought to have gone with her, or made certain that John went. We will have to be very gentle with her, my dear. Very gentle."

"Yes, of course." Mair put her arms around him and let the familiar desire course through her. It was always like that whenever she touched him or thought about him.

"She is so young," James said. "Poor little soul!"

"Come to bed," she whispered.

"Indeed, we must." He looked down at her affectionately. "You will have to take over the children for a few days until Miss Browning is more like herself."

Always other people before herself. Aunt Eliza, Willow Clegg, and now Felice Browning.

"I love you," she said, more loudly than she had intended.

"And I love you," he said at once, pressing her closer. But he was still watching the stairs.

Chapter 5

"And have you decided what you're going to do?" Eliza enquired.

She and Felice sat together, one at each side of the glowing fire in the small cottage. There was warmth in the room which stemmed as much from the kindliness in the older woman's eyes as from the heat of the flames.

In the months since that evening of horror in the woods the small white building had become a refuge. At *Kingsmead* nobody ever referred to what had happened, save in oblique, guarded terms. Eliza had been the only one to mention it openly, without false shame or embarrassing pity. She had met Felice in the village, greeting her with a pleasantly firm, "Miss Browning, I am pleased to find you up and about again. My nephew told me what happened, and you'll not welcome too many questions, but come over to my cottage when the children are out riding, and we'll have coffee and a long talk. No use in holding everything inside yourself, my girl."

Felice had not mean to go, but when Nathan and

Joan were with their father or down at the vicarage, it became unbearable to stay alone in her room or to sit in the parlor with Lady Mair's dark eyes fixed upon her. The gypsies had packed up and moved on, leaving only the circles of their burnt-out fires to remind folk of where they had been. Dr. Evans, who came by once or twice a week, told her she would have nothing more to fear, but he spoke too heartily, and she could not believe him.

Now Aunt Eliza, staring at her out of shrewd, good-humored blue eyes, asked bluntly,

"And have you decided what you're going to do?"

"Lord and Lady Falcon have been most kind," Felice said. "They have assured me that what happened to me makes no difference—"

"And what happens when you give birth to your bastard?" Eliza interrupted bluntly.

The girl stiffened, her fingers clenching on the arms of her chair, her pale face whitening until it was chalk-color. Her eyes, violet-shadowed, were fixed piteously upon a nightmare future.

"That clever young doctor who is setting himself up as Lord Physician of the village isn't as clever as he thinks," Eliza said with an air of triumph. "I can always tell. It's from not having had any of my own, I suppose. When will it be born?"

"March, I think," Felice whispered.

"And the Falcons don't know? Silly question. Of course they don't know, else James would have told me. My dear child, how long do you imagine you can continue to keep it from them?"

"I hoped it might . . . go away," Felice said tremulously.

"Have you done anything to make it go away?" Eliza asked.

"I wondered if you . . ." The blue eyes strayed toward the door at the bottom of the stairs.

"Those potions and herbs are left over from the old days," Eliza said sharply. "I'm not certain if any of them would work, and even if they did you'd not get them from me. Every child, even the bastard, is precious, and has the right to live."

"Like Willow?" Felice ventured.

"Like Willow," Eliza nodded. "She might have been a Falcon, you know, if my elder nephew had married Huldah Clegg, but Fairfax had no mind to wed."

"You were so kind to care for her."

"Ah, well, I always did like young things, growing things," Eliza said. "There was this cottage. My sister Apple, she who was Mair's mother, gave it to me when she ran away to be wed. I brought the babe here and reared her like my own. It has not been easy, for Willow's a shy, wild thing, and Mair doesn't let Nathan or Joan mix with her, but then Mair was always jealous. She'd stop James from coming to see me if she could."

"And what am I to do?" Felice asked, and her hands fell open in despair. "I have no family, no home, no money save what I earn. What am I to do?"

"Hoping the child will go away isn't going to help matters," Eliza said briskly. "You'd best let me have a word with James. He'll not see you turned out without a crust."

"When it was over," Felice said in a tight, strained little voice, "I lay in the grass and hoped that I would die. I kept falling into blackness and I was glad, and then I would wake again, sorry that I was still alive. I don't want this babe, Miss Falcon. I don't want it."

"I told you to call me Aunt Eliza," the other said. "And wanting it or not wanting it has nothing to do with anything. James and I will manage matters between us."

It was not of James that Felice was thinking. His kindness had been something to hold close to her heart, something for which she would always be grateful. But Lady Mair would not be pleased. At the thought of Lady Mair's displeasure, Felice felt sick and dizzy.

She was in her own room, correcting an essay that Nathan had written, when she was summoned to the drawing room. A week had passed since her conversation with Eliza, and most of that time Felice had devoted herself to her pupils and pushed the fear of the coming child to the back of her mind.

Now, trembling a little, she went along the gallery, down the wide staircase and across the hall into the long drawing room which occupied the west wing of the house. It was an elegant apartment, its windows overlooking the smooth lawns which ran clear to the park. Felice averted her eyes hastily, not wishing to remember, and bobbed a curtsey.

"Sit down, Miss Browning. No need to stand on ceremony with us," James invited. His eyes were both admiring and compassionate as they rested upon her. She is, he was thinking, a courageous young woman to have endured such an ordeal without breaking down completely, and to carry such a secret without burdening others with her woes.

"You wished to see me?" Felice sat down on a small high-backed chair and folded her hands together to stop their quivering.

"Is it true that you are with child?" Lady Mair asked abruptly. Her eyes were hard, and two spots of color burned in her cheeks. She sat next to her husband, yet Felice had the impression that a gulf yawned between them.

"It is not your fault," James said swiftly. "What happened to you was a terrible, a shocking thing. The man who would perform such an act is an animal. And such a consequence was always possible. It is not your fault."

"Your aunt told you?"

"Miss Falcon considered that my husband ought to know," Mair said, pressing her lips together. "I am surprised that you did not see fit to confide in me, but we will let that pass."

"Aunt—Miss Falcon guessed," Felice said.

"It's amazing how astute old maids can be," Mair said with a wintry smile. "The child will be born in March, I suppose. I assume you'll not want to keep it."

Until that moment Felice had thought of the child, when she could not helping thinking about it, as a dark and ugly shadow over all her future springtimes. But the other woman's cool, superior tone, the veiled contempt in her eyes, inspired in the governess a flicker of anger.

"I wish to keep the child," she said loudly.

"To keep it? Oh, but have you truly considered—" Mair began.

"All babes are precious," said Felice. "Even bastards." Mentally she blessed Eliza Falcon.

"My dear, what did I tell you?" James exclaimed. "All mothers have a tenderness for their babes. And if you wish to keep your child, Miss Browning, nobody has the right to persuade you out of it."

"All very romantic, and typically masculine," Mair said sharply. "Have you given any thought at all to this? How do you propose to support the child? You can hardly expect to continue to be employed as governesss."

"I had not thought . . ." Felice said, blinking back tears.

"It's fortunate that we are here to take such worries off your mind," James said genially. "For myself, I see no reason why you cannot continue to act as governess, but my wife tells me that would not be quite the, er, thing." He gave Mair an embarrassed, pleading look which she stonily ignored.

"Yes, sir?" Tear-drenched eyes were fixed piteously upon him.

"I have it in mind," James ploughed on, "to put in a tenant at the manor house."

"But it has been empty for years," Mair said. "Ever since Huldah Clegg refused your proposal of marriage and allowed your brother to seduce her."

Her husband flushed deeply, his eyes showing hurt, but his voice remained gentle. "It is not so much a tenant I require as a housekeeper," he said. "I need somebody to look after the place, to live there and keep it clean and warm. Miss Browning, I think that you and your babe might be very comfortable there. It is not a large house, and we could get a little maid from the village to help you."

"I imagine that Miss Browning could manage the work very adequately," Mair said coldly. "She would hardly presume further upon your generosity. As it is, there will be a great scandal in the neighborhood."

"Are you certain that you would want me at the manor?" Felice asked. Gratitude and relief were bubbling up in her. In her dreams Lord Falcon rode a great white horse and his hands were tender. Sometimes she pictured those hands reaching out for her, but then a shutter closed down in her mind. The episode in the wood had killed something in her nature, so that for the rest of her life she would be condemned to dream childish, romantic dreams.

"It would be too lonely for a woman on her own," Mair said.

"We can hire a groom, if Miss Browning is nervous," James said.

"A maid and a groom," Mair exclaimed bitterly. "Many girls in your position would have been turned out."

"My dear, Miss Browning cannot be held responsible," James said.

"There is an old belief," Mair said, "that no woman is raped unless she invites it." Even she was shocked by the cruelty of her words, and she colored in shame, though she still held her head high.

"My dear, it is not like you to be unjust," James reproved her quietly. The color flamed more brilliantly in her cheeks, and she dropped her eyes, hating the violence of her own feelings, hating the reproach in her husband's face, hating the meek blue eyes of the governess.

"I would have died," she said fiercely, "before I would have let any man put his hands upon me."

"You were always strong," James said, as if excusing a fault in her. "Miss Browning has not your strength, my dear. And she is very young. She is our responsibility."

"Yes, of course." The violence had drained out of her, and her voice was dull. Responsibility and duty were James's watchwords. Everyone who excited his compassion joined his list of dependents. And all that remained for his wife was affection where she craved passion, gentleness and understanding when she needed him to shout at her, to shake her, to crush her to him and smother her doubts with the weight of his lean, hard body.

"I think I'll go out for a while," she said abruptly. "If Miss Browning intends to take your most generous offer, then there is little point in our continuing the discussion. Where are the children?"

"Nathan is upstairs, working on his map of Africa," Felice said. "Joan went out into the garden. I asked her to find me twelve different types of grasses for our nature study." She spoke quickly, placating, her hands still trembling, her eyes turned in James's direction.

They are in love, whispered the jealous imp in Mair's mind. He does not know it, does not recognize it yet, but already she has a claim on his protection, and she is grateful to him. She left the room briskly, her heels tapping on the polished floor between the rich rugs.

"You must not think my wife does not feel great sympathy for you," James was saying. "This affair has upset her more than she will admit."

Mair gritted her teeth and passed on into the kitchen at the other side of the great hall. The sight of one of the maids dozing by the range further irritated her nerves, and she banged a skillet down loudly on the table before stalking through the back door. The stables had once been joined to the house, but since the building of the east wing the horses were lodged beyond a high wall that separated barns and outbuildings from the kitchen gardens and orchard.

Joan was neither in the garden nor the orchard. Mair cupped her hands to her mouth and called, and heard in reply her daughter's answering voice raised shrilly beyond the trees.

"Joan! You have no business to wander away from

the house!" Mair exclaimed crossly, hurrying in the direction of the piping call.

Joan was pressed against the trunk of an elm, her hands over her eyes. As her mother stepped closer over the uneven ground, she called again, high and excited.

"We're playing peek-a-boo! It's my turn to find her."

"To find whom?" Mair began, and stopped as Willow Clegg stepped out from behind another tree.

The girl wore her usual green gown, its hem ragged, its loose folds blending with the fading colors of the early autumn foliage. Her pale hair hung in silky strands at each side of her narrow face, and her pointed chin jutted defiantly.

"What are you doing here?" Mair asked sharply. "Who gave you permission to come onto Falcon land?"

"I often come here," Willow said in her sweet, clear voice. "This is my uncle's land. Aunt Eliza told me that if matters had been different I might have lived at *Kingsmead*, at the big house."

"We're playing peek-a-boo," Joan called again. She lowered her hands and looked uncertainly between her mother and the other girl.

"This is Falcon land," Mair said again. "I forbid you to come here. I forbid you to speak to Joan."

"Joan is my cousin," Willow said, and for the first time something of a child's bewilderment sounded in her voice. "Joan and Nathan are both my cousins."

"No bastard claims kinship with my children," Mair said. Anger was rising in her again, an anger that stemmed from many causes held to herself since her marriage, festering deep in her nature. At that instant Willow Clegg was not simply the unwanted niece, but the child that might have been James's daughter had he married Huldah Clegg.

"You should go back to the big house," Willow said. "My uncle is there, isn't he? With the governess?" Her eyes, pale and down-slanting under thick, fair lashes, were sly and spiteful.

Mair opened her mouth to speak, but a red mist was closing in about her. Her hand groped behind her on the ground, though she was not conscious of having stooped. It closed about something heavy and jagged. Somewhere in the redness Joan called out on a high, frightened note. Some figure blurred across her vision, and then the jagged, heavy object left her hand, arching through the air, and something else thudded and was still.

The mist cleared slowly and it was cold. Mair walked slowly over to where Willow knelt and looked down at the feathery tail and the bloodied head of the old dog.

"Beau was my mother's," Willow said. "He was a puppy when I was born, and now he's old. He's old and he couldn't run fast. He never hurt anybody in his whole life. He never hurt anybody at all."

"But I didn't intend—" Mair began. She was shaking as if she stood in a high wind. Near to the dead dog the stone she had flung lay inanimate, its power spent.

"You killed my mother's dog," Willow said. "You killed Beau. You killed Beau." She sprang at the older woman, her face a mask of fury, her long nails ripping at Mair's clothes. Mair twisted away and heard, above Joan's bewildered sobbing, the ripping of her gown.

From Willow there came a long, drawn-out gasp. The younger girl had ceased her frantic onslaught and was staring at Mair's leg, which, bared to the thigh, revealed a purple crescent moon on the firm flesh.

"The devil's kiss," Willow breathed. "You have it on your leg, as I do."

"A birthmark," Mair said. "It's only a birthmark."

"A witch mark," the girl contradicted. "Aunt Eliza told me about it, about the purple crescent that appears from time to time on the leg of a Falcon woman. She who bears the mark can learn the curse, the words of the curse which was put upon our family long ago. My aunt could never tell me those words for she doesn't have the mark, but she told me that her sister Apple had it, and Apple was your mother. She must have given you the words!"

"She never did," Mair said.

"You're lying!" Willow flashed. "You do know the words. I know you do! And I have the right to know them, too. My father was a Falcon, and I have the right—"

"You're a bastard and have no rights," Mair said. She pulled her torn skirt over the telltale mark and went to where Joan stood crying, her round face streaked with tears. As she picked up the child, holding her closely, Willow said pleadingly, "Tell me the words. Please tell them to me. I'll not bother you, nor trespass again. Only tell me the words, please?"

"I'll tell you nothing. Get off my husband's land, or I'll take a horsewhip to you!" Mair shouted. Willow stood for a moment longer, her hands held out. For an instant Mair had the curious impression that an older girl stood there, a girl who begged for acceptance and understanding. Then Joan began to cry again noisily, and she hugged her tightly and went back toward the house. The pleading died out of Willow's eyes and her hands fell to her sides again. She stood very still, watching Mair's tall figure diminishing among the trees, and her eyes were opaque, their pupils slitted.

Then she bent down and picked up the dog. The body was still warm, the blood coagulating around the ear. She buried her face briefly in the silky fur and then went slowly away, across the open meadows which sloped down toward the cottage.

She scraped a deep hole with a piece of broken fencing and buried the dog, pushing back the disturbed clods of earth with small, industrious hands. When the ground was smooth again she rose from her knees, shaking back the tangles of hair. There was a suffocating weight on her chest; the very air seemed tinged with some poisonous miasma. Some part of her struggled against it, tried to hold to the gentleness of the affection that had been between Beau and herself. But it was much easier to let the blackness flood in, to breathe the evil until it was sweet as honey flooding her soul.

It had taken much longer than she thought to bury the dog. It was growing dusk, and the tops of the grasses were tinged with blue. The wind blew chill with the approach of autumn and there was sadness in the keening of the birds. Above the horizon a sickle moon threatened the emerging stars.

Willow wrapped her arms about herself and ran, fleet-footed, into the trees. The glow of candlelight came from the unshuttered windows of the cottage, and Aunt Eliza called from the open door, "Willow! Your supper's ready if you want it."

The girl went in, blinking as the light of candles and fire dazzled her. Eliza was cutting into a pie and the fragrance of cinnamon rose to Willow's nostrils.

"You're late child. It's not wise to roam about in the dark," she said.

"After what happened to the governess?" Willow asked.

"You're not supposed to know about that," Aunt Eliza replied.

"I know nearly everything about everybody," Willow said calmly, helping herself to a piece of pie. "The governess is going to have a baby, and that is why the gypsies packed up and went away so quickly. And I heard Uncle James telling you that he meant to ask her to be housekeeper at the manor. Wasn't the manor meant for my own mother once?"

"James furnished it for her," Aunt Eliza admitted, "but your mother refused to wed him."

"Because his brother had already got her with child, with me," Willow said. "If she had married Uncle James, I would have been born in the manor house, wouldn't I?"

"It was not to be," Eliza said. "In the end we must accept what comes to us and make the best of it."

"Do we?" Willow swallowed the last crumb of pie and licked her fingers, glancing at the older woman out of the corner of her eyes.

"I'm sorry for that poor girl," Aunt Eliza said. "To be forced against one's will—I declare I don't know what the world is coming to! At least you can be sure that you were born out of love. Your mother loved your father very much."

"But Fairfax Falcon didn't love her enough to marry her," Willow said in a low voice.

"Well, I loved you enough to rear you," Aunt Eliza said cheerfully. "Drink your milk. That new doctor says milk is nourishing, though I doubt it myself, except for babes and old folk, of course. Where's Beau? I have a shin bone for him."

"Beau's dead," Willow said.

"Dead?" Aunt Eliza echoed the word blankly. "Beau dead?"

"He fell down and died," Willow said. "Just fell down and died. I buried him in the meadow."

"Oh, my dear, I'm so sorry," Eliza said. "I'm so very sorry."

"He was old," Willow said casually. "He couldn't run fast any more. I was going to ask Uncle James to have him put down anyway."

"And you do have the pony that Uncle James gave you," Aunt Eliza said, eyeing the girl uncertainly.

"Yes." Willow drank her milk sedately. After a minute she looked up and said in the same sweetly indifferent voice, "Uncle James is very kind. He gave me a pony and lets me live here with you. And he lets the governess live at the manor house. That new baby is going to be very fortunate, don't you think so, Aunt Eliza dear?"

Chapter 6

"A very pretty girl child, black-haired and blue-eyed like her mother," Dr. Evans told Mair.

"I suppose that I ought to go over and see her," Mair said guiltily. "One should set an example in these matters, and it was not, after all, Miss Browning's fault."

"But you would have preferred her to leave the village." He made it a statement, not a question, his eyes shrewd.

"She insisted upon keeping the babe," Mair said. "I cannot blame her, for it's natural for a mother to love her children. But if she had gone away, she could have told people she was a widow. I even suggested to my husband that we pay her a small allowance, but he refused. He said that we have a personal responsibility toward those we employ."

"That sounds like Lord Falcon," the doctor said.

"My husband is a very kind and generous man," Mair said defiantly.

"As I have every reason to know. Without his help I could never have set up a practice here."

"I wish more people would come to you," Mair said, "but most folk prefer to doctor their own hurts, or drive to Maidstone for any serious complaint. You must find Marie Regina exceedingly dull after the excitements of the city."

"There are occasions when I don't find it dull at all," he said. His gaze admired her, and she could not resist a little stirring of pleasure. He was not, of course, the kind of man who could attract her, being very far from gentlemanly, but to have overcome his background sufficiently to have entered the medical profession surely entitled him to come consideration. She smiled at him warmly across the width of the parlor, conscious that she was looking her best in a loose robe of dark red which flattered her dark brown hair and brown eyes.

"She is calling the babe Caroline," the doctor said as the silence threatened to become uneasy.

"Caroline Browning." Mair tasted the syllables on her tongue and found them sour.

"I shall be calling on Miss Browning in a day or two," he said, "if you should require an escort."

"I need none," she said briefly.

"Company then?" He spoke softly, the gypsy in him very evident in his face.

"In a week or two. I'll ride over to the manor in a week or two, when Miss Browning is stronger. It's so inconsiderate of people to crowd to see a new babe before the mother is fully recovered from her confinement."

"I hardly think Miss Browning is bothered with too many visitors," Dr. Evans said wryly.

"My husband has been to see her twice," Mair said, shifting a little as if her chair was uncomfortable. "He speaks of taking Nathan and Joan to see the new baby. As if it hasn't been difficult enough to explain to them why Miss Browning went to live in the manor house at all. As for the child—Nathan understands a little, I think. Joan thinks babies grow under gooseberry bushes, but she has noticed that there is usually a husband there."

"It will be a nine-days wonder," he reassured her.

"As long as people don't think we were remiss in our duty toward her," Mair said.

"Neither you nor Lord Falcon could have done more," he told her. "And Miss Eliza Falcon has been a tower of strength."

"Old maids have a great fondness for poking their noses into other folks' affairs," Mair said. "She has been sleeping up in the manor, you know, she and the girl. And even Uncle Weston bestirred himself this morning to ride over with a lace shawl he's been embroidering."

"And milady's nose is out of joint," Dr. Evans said, gazing innocently into space.

"You presume too far—" Mair began, but laughter welled up in her, cleansing the resentment, and her face sparkled suddenly. It had been a long time since anybody had caused her to feel genuine amusement at herself, and though he had overstepped the bounds of propriety she felt a warmth toward him. At least he did not rush off to see the governess and her bastard brat, but sat with her in the snug parlor at *Kingsmead*, treating her as if she were a desirable woman. Imperceptibly, under the folds of crimson silk, her limbs relaxed, and her strong, shapely hands inched along the arms of her chair, smoothing the leather as if it were warm flesh.

Weston Falcon, having presented the shawl and admired the baby, was constrained to accept a glass of sherry from the hands of his sister. He and Eliza had seldom met in the years since she had gone to live at the cottage, and in their youth they had never been close, but now some impulse made him say, "Only two of us left now, out of all our family. Those were happy days when the six of us were together."

"Happy? Is that how you remember them?" Eliza looked astonished. "Have you forgotten how it was when our father was alive? Have you forgotten that Helen and Apple ran away to be wed, that Prescott was forced into marriage with a girl who didn't love him, that Nat was tricked into the army and killed at Bunker Hill? Have you forgotten that Mother hanged herself?"

"I see no reason to dwell on unpleasant things," Weston said, his plump cheeks sagging into sulky folds. "You chose to take the Clegg child and live in the cottage. Nobody forced you."

"And I have never regretted it," Eliza said firmly. "Willow's a Falcon, for all that Mair won't acknowledge her."

"Where is the girl?" Weston glanced about him.

"She comes and goes," Eliza said. "You cannot fetter a wild thing. She runs as she chooses and comes home when she is hungry. Have you finished that sherry? There's more if you want it."

"I dare not." He set down the glass regretfully. "My digestion is not what it was."

"If you took more exercise instead of lurking in your bedroom, your digestion would improve," Eliza said unsympathetically. "Miss Browning is recovering so nicely that I shall have her on her feet in a day or two. And then Willow and I can get back to the cottage." She was bustling him out of the parlor, anxious to get on with her work. Practical, energetic

Eliza! He stifled a sigh, feeling elderly and tired in the face of her vitality.

Eliza began to tidy the parlor vigorously. Weston, she conceded, had been kind to come, but he irritated her with his fussy, effeminate mannerisms. She sensed that he was afraid of Mair, afraid of causing discord in the big house where he had lived out his amiable, useless existence. When she had tidied the room she went upstairs again, and sat, knitting needles clicking, by the high bed where Felice, frail and pretty after her ordeal, lay propped on starched pillows. The new baby slept in the carved cradle at the foot of the bed, dark lashes feathering the round cheeks, black head quiescent.

It is odd, Eliza thought, that bastard babes are often fairer than those born in wedlock. Willow was exquisite when she was tiny, like a fairy child.

"It was very kind of Mr. Falcon to bring the shawl," Felice said.

"I never thought him to have so much energy," Eliza said drily.

"And Lord Falcon has said he will bring Nathan and Joan to see the baby."

"So he did." The knitting needles clicked more busily, and Eliza's head bent lower over her work. So the poor child fancies herself in love with James. It was evident in the way she brought his name into her conversation, in the shy, bright color that mantled her face. But my nephew loves that jealous Welsh cousin he married, Eliza thought with sadness. He is never likely even to contemplate infidelity. Aloud she said, "Lady Mair will probably bring the children. She has kept away, I think, for fear of tiring you with too many visitors."

"There have not been many," the girl said.

"People will come and see you very soon," Eliza soothed. "What happened to you might have happened to one of their own daughters, and for that reason alone they will sympathize with you. And soon they will forget, and only think how pretty the babe is and how brave you are to keep her. Why, one day a handsome young man might come riding into Marie Regina, seeking a pretty wife."

"Fairy tales," said the girl, and she spoke with a kind of wistful bitterness. "I don't believe in fairy tales anymore."

In the garden Weston was frowning at the small, slight figure who stood, green-gowned, before him. Willow's hair was neatly combed, her feet respectably shod, and there was no reason in the world why her slanting eyes should make him feel uneasy.

"You came to see Miss Browning's baby," she said sweetly. "It's to be called Caroline, and is to live here at the manor house. The manor house was furnished ready for my mother, you know, but she had me and then she died. And I live in the cottage with Aunt Eliza."

"I know."

"You never ride over to see us," she said, gently implacable. "Why don't you ride over to see us, Uncle Weston?"

"I'm very busy," he said. "Very busy, indeed."

"And would you have come to see us if we lived here at the manor house?" she persisted.

"I really cannot tell, child," he said uncomfortably. "You must not ask so many questions. It is not well-bred in a little girl to ask so many questions."

"But I am a bastard," she replied serenely. "A bastard isn't expected to be well-bred, Uncle Weston."

"I wish you would not call me Uncle Weston," he said irritably.

"But you are my uncle," Willow said. "My great-uncle, to be exact, as Aunt Eliza is my great-aunt. We are all related, you see, though Lady Mair will not have it so. I think she is jealous of me, because Uncle James once wanted to marry my mother. Did you know my mother?"

He nodded slowly, remembering Huldah Clegg, a tall, wide-shouldered girl with hair like wheat and eyes that sought the far horizons. Restless Huldah.

"And my father? You knew him, of course. He was your nephew, and elder brother to Uncle James."

"Of course."

Fairfax, tall and handsome, powerfully charming, remorsefully weak. Fairfax had cared nothing for the land he was to inherit. He had seduced Huldah Clegg, apparently out of some fancy born on a summer's day, and then he deserted her, leaving her to bear her child alone.

"Your father was not a worthy man," Weston said at last. "And your mother was—she was a very foolish young woman. Running about with her skirts tucked up and that damned dog everlastingly at her heels."

"Beau?" Willow was suddenly very still and quiet.

"That's the name. Frisky, gambolling thing. I prefer cats, myself."

"Shall I get your horse for you?" she enquired. "It's in the stable."

"Thank you." Wondering a little at the abrupt turn in the conversation, he watched her run lightly around the corner of the house. Odd little thing! She made him feel uncomfortable, conscious of his balding fair head, his tightly corseted paunch, his dimpled hands.

It was cold for the start of April; hoarfrost still sparkled on the grass. The manor house, smaller than *Kingsmead,* was red-ivied, warm, and secure, its windows reflecting pale gleams of timid sunlight. The house had stood as long as its eager neighbor, belonging first to the Astons and then to the Fleets. The first owner of the manor was the aunt of Lady Alys Falcon, wife of the second Henry Falcon. In fact, for nearly three hundred years Aston and Fleet women had been wedding Falcon men, until with the marriage of his own father to Joanna Fleet the two estates had been merged.

It was a friendly house, rosebushes spiking its lawn, daffodils and crocuses pushing up through the hard earth. James had prepared the manor for the reception of his intended, Huldah Clegg, but Huldah had never gone there as a bride, and it had stood empty since, until the arrival of the pretty little governess and her hedge-get.

"I've brought your horse," Willow said, approaching from the stables.

He fumbled in his pocket for a coin and, finding none, mounted weightily, gathering the reins up in his plump hands. He felt tired and slightly breathless, a trifle apprehensive of Mair's reaction when he arrived back at *Kingsmead.* She had never liked Felice Browning and she would approve even less of his having visited her. He was not even certain why he had bothered to come since Miss Browning's eyes had filled with tears when he presented her with the shawl, and his sister had plainly thought him something of a nuisance.

He nodded curtly to the slight, green-clad figure and, shifting his weight, kicked his heels against his mount's sides. That instant the animal let out a scream of pain, reared and bucked, lashing out furiously with its hind legs. Manor house, frosty grass, bare rose-bushes, and gravel path whirled and spun around him, and then he was falling, slowly at first, and then faster and faster into a black pit.

"In the name of Heaven, what was that?" Eliza, tangled knitting clutched in her hand, darted through the front door, her grey hair escaping wildly from the edges of her mobcap.

Willow had seized the horse's reins and was apparently adjusting the saddle. The beast stood trembling, the whites of its eyes showing. Weston Falcon lay at a grotesque angle, blood congealing in his ear, his eyes open to the pale sky.

"Weston! Weston!" Eliza was on her knees feeling for pulse and heartbeat. When she looked up her face was drawn with shock.

"What happened? Willow, what happened?" she questioned urgently.

"The horse reared up and threw him," Willow said in her sweet voice. "I suppose he wasn't used to riding and couldn't keep his seat."

"Take your own pony and ride for Dr. Evans," the older woman ordered. "Tell him there's been an accident, and then go on to the big house. Tell James —oh! but he is in Maidstone today. Tell Lady Mair what has happened. Hurry!"

"I'll ride this horse," Willow said, springing nimbly to its back. "It won't throw me." She cantered down the drive before Eliza could raise any objections. As she rounded the bend she tossed away the prickly burr which, hidden under the saddle, had maddened the horse under Weston's heavy bulk.

She was at the main gates when she saw Dr. Evans riding toward her along the road with a red-cloaked figure at his side. Checking her own mount, she sat waiting quietly until they drew abreast.

Mair's face under its red hood set into grim lines as she beheld the slim, childish figure. She had succeeded in putting the girl out of her mind in the months that has passed since their last meeting, and it was unpleasant to have to meet her again.

Dr. Evans, who had seen Willow about the manor house and considered her an eccentric, badly reared child, nodded curtly. Fair girls were not to his taste, and this one was too young, anyway. Mature women who resembled himself in coloring were those who woke the lust in his carefully civilized nature.

"Are you going to the manor house?" Willow asked.

"I decided to visit Miss Browning and the baby," Mair said, and was immediately annoyed with herself for having vouchsafed an explanation. Willow always made her feel clumsy and old, no longer Lady Falcon of *Kingsmead* but Mair Price who had grown up on a Welsh farm and come south to marry a cousin still in love with a dead woman. At the back of Mair's mind lay the tormenting conviction that when James looked at Willow he saw in her some trace of Huldah Clegg.

"The doctor had better go to the manor house, too," Willow said.

"Miss Browning isn't sick, is she?" he asked sharply. "She and the babe were fine when I called on them last."

"It's Mr. Falcon," Willow said. "My Uncle Weston, you know. He was thrown from his horse."

"That's Mr. Falcon's horse you're riding now!" Mair exclaimed.

"I borrowed him so that I could come and find the doctor. He's quite calm again now."

"Is Mr. Falcon badly hurt?" Dr. Evans asked.

"He's dead," Willow said simply. "He was thrown onto the gravel and hit his head against a stone. Stones are dangerous things, aren't they?" Her eyes flickered toward Mair.

"I'll see what's to be done." The gypsy in Evans vanished and gave place to the cool, professional man as he spurred his mount up the drive. Mair gave Willow a glance in which shock and doubt and loathing were intermingled, and galloped after him.

It was after twilight when Willow came back to the manor house. The body of Weston Falcon had already been taken back to *Kingsmead*.

James was red-eyed and white-faced. He wept over his uncle, unable to believe that the vague, kindly man who had always been part of his life had died so violently, so suddenly.

"He was not so old," he said over and over. "I cannot imagine how he came to be thrown. Jester is usually so gentle. Poor Uncle Weston! Poor fellow!" Above all things James hated change in those about him. Even the ruin of a fence or a barn induced in him an intense melancholy. He could not bear the thought of death for those whom he loved.

Eliza, having settled Felice and the babe for the night, came down into the kitchen. There would have to be a wake, and she intended to supply some of the pies and puddings with which the mourners would restore themselves.

The fire still burned cheerfully in the parlor grate but she could not sit still. It was a sad irony that, on the very day she and her brother had talked for the first time in years, he should have met his death.

Willow came in through the back door, her hair loose about her shoulders, a fine spattering of rain staining her green dress. Her eyes were shining, as if tears stood in them, but her voice had its usual demure timbre.

"Are they all gone?"

"Some time past. Where have you been, child?"

"I went over to the meadow to see where Beau is buried," Willow said. "There's grass all over again now, and nowhere to mark the place."

"But why didn't you come home?" Eliza asked in concern. "And to run out in this weather with no shawl or cloak!"

"I don't feel the cold," Willow said, "and I don't want to intrude."

"My dear, Weston was your great-uncle just as he was Nathan's and Joan's," Eliza said gently. "Haven't I always taught you to regard yourself as a Falcon? And isn't your Uncle James kind to you?"

"He is kind to everybody," Willow said, "even to Miss Browning and her babe. As you are kind."

"Me? Nonsense!"

"You came here to help out until the governess is better," Willow pointed out. "And you took care of me, didn't you?"

"The two things are quite different," Eliza said. "Poor Miss Browning has nobody in the world. I help her out of pity. But I always wanted a little girl of my own, and you have been that little girl."

"I am not so little," Willow said.

"You'll be a young lady soon," Eliza agreed. "Then you'll have to stop running about the district like a goosegirl, I suppose. Sometimes I think I ought to have reared you more strictly, but I know how I felt when I was a girl. I hated to wear dresses and walk like a lady with my toes turned out. So I let you grow up as Nature intended, and I only hope that I have done right. The parson has grave doubts."

"Bother the parson!" Willow blew him off the palm of her hand. "Is there anything for supper?"

"There's some cold beef in the pantry and the rest of the lemon meringue. These pies are for the funeral supper. I couldn't settle to anything, and grief or no grief, folk have to eat." Eliza blinked suddenly, a tear sliding down her nose and plopping into the pastry.

"He was my brother," she said. "He was always very foolish, I'm afraid, but he and I were the only ones left of our generation."

"He died very quickly," Willow said, rummaging in the pantry and emerging with a chunk of beef in one hand and a slice of meringue in the other. "He died very quickly."

"God be thanked," Eliza said.

"Oh, yes indeed." Willow's small face was gentle. "We must indeed thank Him for small mercies."

"Go and sit by the fire. I'll join you when these are in the oven," Eliza said.

Willow, in her neat graceful fashion, walked across the hall into the parlor. She had no desire now to live in the manor house, though as a child she had frequently peered through the windows at the shrouded furniture and imagined how it would have been if her mother had wed Uncle James. But now the house was full of the silly governess and her baby. Willow wanted to go back home to the cottage.

She went over to the window and leaned her thin elbows on the windowsill. The garden was dim and blue-grey, the gushes twisting into night shapes, a wind crooning to the frost-glinting grass.

"Poor Uncle Weston," she said sadly. "Such a dreadful way to die." And her mouth curved into another gentle smile.

PART II
1822

Chapter 7

Snow lay white and crisp over the fields surrounding
Marie Regina. In the hollow that spread itself between
sloping graveyard and ruin-crowned hill, the village
wound icy cobbles toward the green, which was now
a white blanket on which lads flung snowballs. The
river itself was frozen, and only the marks of skates
patterned its virgin surface. Against the pearl sky bare
branches reached up quivering in the chill breeze that
eddied round the remaining leaves, scattering them in
disconsolate heaps.

New Year's was the time of year that Willow loved
best. Christmas had never meant very much to her,
for neither she nor Aunt Eliza went to church, a
custom that had long ceased to scandalize the vicar,
who tolerantly accepted the situation as another example of Miss Falcon's eccentricity. "I endured so much
church-going when I was a girl," Eliza said, "that I
decided I'd give myself permanent holiday as soon
as I could please myself. It shocks the good folk of the
village, of course, but I've a notion one can worship the
Lord anywhere."

To please James she sent Willow to church two or three times a year, and once a week told her charge stories from the Bible, but Willow had flatly refused to attend services after she was ten, and the Bible stories had lapsed at the same time. Willow thought that God was not at all the Loving Father folk said He was. There was no use in saying prayers to a waxy doll in a crib, nor to the badly carved figure hanging on the cross above the altar. There was more sense in the terrible Jehovah of the Old Testament, who went about turning people into salt and waging war against rival gods. In such conflicts Willow's sympathies were all with the rival gods, a fact that would have distressed Eliza who, despite her neglect of conventional church-going, had retained all the lovely simplicity of her childhood beliefs.

But there was, on the night that the old year merged into the new, a sense of worship in the girl's soul that had nothing to do with church or creed. On this night the longing to be free of all that limited her powers was like a fever in her blood.

She had been to the graveyard to put a spray of Christmas roses on the Falcon tomb. This was usually Aunt Eliza's yearly offering, but the older woman had slipped on an icy step the previous week and was, to her disgust, confined to the fireside until her sprained ankle should heal.

Willow, green cloak and hood enveloping her slight frame, laid the flowers dutifully at the feet of the stone angel and grinned at the stern, carven features. Much use a threatening sword against the forces she intended to invoke!

She had grown scarcely at all since her twelfth birthday, and at sixteen and a half her face still had the grave concentration of a child. Only her eyes, down-slanting and blank as water, were ancient.

She turned away from the ornate monument and scrambled up toward the low wall beyond which the girl Catrin lay lonely in her unhallowed grave. The headstone was obscured by drifts of snow, but she had no need to read the words in order to remind herself of the tale. Poor Catrin, wed to a Falcon and swum to her death because she bore the devil's kiss upon her thigh.

"I wonder," Willow said loudly, "if you knew the words of the curse. I wonder if you would tell them to me."

The silence around her was as deep as the snow. Up there, above the church and the village, there was a purity in the air. She breathed it deeply into her lungs and raised her head, pushing back the hood and shaking free the long, pale strands of hair.

"Pretty hair," commented a voice from the other side of the wall. "Hair like that could bind a man's heart, or strangle him."

The woman who rose up from behind the tombstones wore the gay, tattered plaid of a gypsy. She was neither young nor old but in her middle years, when the last flames of beauty rise up in a final tribute to desire.

"You ought not to creep up on folk like that," Willow said sharply.

"I've been sitting here," the woman said, her voice whining, "trying to summon the strength to call out."

"You look healthy to me," Willow said, and her eyes narrowed.

"I've a sickness of the spirit, daughter." The woman moved slowly to the wall and sat down heavily. Her

fine, dark eyes were brilliant, the color in her high
cheekbones vivid scarlet.

"Oh." Willow, who was not much interested in sickness of the spirit, gave a barely concealed yawn.

"My name is Sarah," the woman said. "I'm not from
these parts, not from any parts really. I'm a travelling
woman."

"A gypsy?"

"My mother was pure Romany," the woman said,
"but she took up with a traveling man, a tinker out of
Donegal. Her tribe would have nought to do with her
after that, and I was reared on the move, as it were.
Ah, they're gone now, and my own man is dead, and
I've a mind to discover my mother's people and see if
there's ones among them who will call me cousin."

"There are no gypsies here," Willow said. "They
used to camp up on the common every summer, but
nearly four summers ago one of them attacked a girl,
and now they don't come."

"And would that girl have had a child?" Sarah
asked. "A little girl."

Eyeing the woman thoughtfully, Willow enquired,
"Do you know about it?"

"The man who did the deed," Sarah said, "was my
son."

"Your son! But you said—"

"I cannot tell the truth to a stranger at first glance,"
Sarah said, "but you have a kind face, my dear. A
trustful face. The man was my son. Simpleminded he
was, but very strong, very cunning. My mother's people let him travel with them sometimes, and after
he'd been on the road a few months he'd come home
to me. But one year he didn't come home. I went in
search of him up and down the country, and then I
met up with my mother's people. They told me he'd

attacked a young lady and so they hanged him—
hanged my son and threw him to the fishes. That's a
terrible thing for a mother to hear."

"I'm very sorry," Willow said politely.

"But if there's a child—" The dark eyes fixed themselves upon her imploringly. "I'd give the world to
see my grandchild. Just to see it for a few minutes."

"I know where the child is," Willow said slowly.

"I'd give you—"

"What would you give me?"

"My earrings?" The woman pulled back her shawl
to display heavy gold circles.

"I don't wear earrings," Willow said loftily.

"A charm, then? I have a charm that belonged to
my mother. You can have the charm." She withdrew a
brown hand from the folds of her skirt and held it
out palm upward to display a smooth black stone that
reflected dark fire in its depths.

"It is sacred to Lilith," the woman said in a low
voice. "She who was Adam's wife and stole away
his soul long before Eve was made. She is goddess
of the dark side of the moon."

Willow's pale eyes reflected twin stones in their
slitted pupils. A queer little tremor ran through her,
as if a splinter of ice had lodged at the base of her
spine. She had no idea whether the woman spoke the
truth or not. It was possible she had been sent to steal
the child. Gypsies did sometimes steal children, it was
rumored. It might be amusing to let it happen and
have the whole district in an uproar. On the other
hand, it was equally possible that her own part in the
affair might be discovered.

"I'll take the charm," she said, but the brown
hand clenched and the darkly gleaming thing was
hidden.

"Show me the child first," Sarah said.

Willow's eyes clouded in concentration. She wanted the charm more than she had ever wanted anything in her life, but she knew intuitively that the woman would not be content with merely seeing the child.

"We'll have to wait until after dark," she said at last, thinking rapidly. "Miss Browning—that's the woman who was attacked—lives at the manor house with the child. There's no man on the place and only one little deaf girl to act as servant. I know how to get in the back way."

"I can meet you," the woman said eagerly.

"By the bridge, around eight o'clock. Can you wait until then?"

"I can wait."

"And you'll give me the charm?"

"Yes, of course." The dark eyes flickered slightly, and Willow knew that the woman had lied.

"By the bridge, then. At eight," she repeated, and ran swiftly across the snowy field. When she glanced back the gaudy figure had disappeared among the tombstones once more. Through the long afternoon Willow pictured her sitting there, pressed down behind the snow-covered stone. The gypsy had looked feverish. The intense cold would surely do her no good. Perhaps she would lack the strength to reach the bridge, and then the gleaming black stone would never lie in Willow's small palm.

"Child, you're never going out!" Eliza exclaimed as Willow reached for cloak and hood again.

"Only for an hour or two. It's a clear night."

"But icy cold. You'll catch your death—"

"You know I never catch cold," Willow said calmly. "I thought I'd ride over to the manor house to see Miss Browning."

"But you never go and see Miss Browning. Why to-night?"

"Because it's New Year's Eve and I am full of the milk of human kindness"

Grateful for the injury to her aunt's ankle which had prevented her from learning that the vicar had already invited Miss Browning and little Caroline to supper that evening, Willow unlatched the cottage door.

The clearing was already moonlit and snow spangled the dark bushes. Further off strange, grumbling noises came from the river as it flowed under its sheet of ice. She had already considered and discarded the possibility of pushing the gypsy into the river; the woman was tall, and she might make an outcry even if Willow succeeded in luring her to the bank.

"I'll be back in time to see the Old Year out with you," she promised sweetly, and went to the stable built onto the side of the cottage to get her pony. She had no particular affection for the animal, Beau and Aunt Eliza being the only creatures for whom she had ever felt love. There were times when she came near to loving Uncle James, but then she remembered whom he had married, and the impulse died.

Now, mounted on her uncle's gift, she rode serenely up the narrow bridle path to the main road and saw, leaning against the bridge, the figure of the gypsy, color draining from the bright, ragged garments, gold earrings glinting under the black hair.

"You're late. The church clock is near nine," the woman accused.

"That clock has been wrong since the vicar had it put there," Willow said. "You look cold."

"I'm frozen to the marrow," the gypsy said, a whine

creeping into her voice. "Not a bite to eat, nor a drop to drink since this morning!"

"I've some whisky." Willow patted the saddlebag invitingly.

The woman reached eagerly for the bottle, tilting it to her mouth greedily. "It's good. Very good," she pronounced at length.

"Take some more," Willow offered. The woman took another swig and then stoppered the bottle firmly. "Too much liquor isn't good on an empty stomach," she said. "I've no mind to fall down in my cups and freeze to death by the roadside. You promised to show me my grandchild."

"Have you a horse?"

"I took a ride on the coach for as far as I could afford and walked the rest."

Willow thought it more likely that the woman had left her mount concealed somewhere, ready for a speedy exit.

"You'd best ride with me," she said aloud. "We cross the bridge and turn in at the manor gates. It's not very far."

The woman mounted slowly. Evidently she had spoken truly when she complained of weakness, or perhaps, as Willow hoped, the whisky had already dulled her senses a little.

They trotted slowly over the bridge, unseen save by the occasional nighthawk who swooped and dived, spreading black wings against the moon.

Miss Browning and the child would have been safely installed in the vicarage since before dark, so there was no danger of meeting them along the path. Nevertheless, there had been, Willow thought, a certain amount of good fortune attendant upon her scheme. The gypsy, for reasons of her own, had preferred to remain out of sight and had evidently not seen anybody driving from the direction of the manor.

Only a faint light gleamed from an upper window. The little deaf girl, who did the rough work at the manor, was probably warming the beds in readiness for Miss Browning's return.

"We have to go round to the back," Willow said, wishing her fellow-rider would not grip her so tightly. "There's a door there that leads into the cellar."

"Won't it be locked?"

"I have a key," Willow hissed as they rounded the corner of the house.

It was dark there, the light from the window obscured, the moon fled briefly behind a cloud. Willow dismounted and felt, rather than saw, the shape of her companion at her side.

"Give me the key," the woman said. She sounded eager and urgent.

"The black stone first." Willow retreated a step and held out her hand.

"What would a pretty little thing like you do with an amulet of Lilith?" the woman asked.

"That's my business," Willow said.

"Here it is, then." The woman pressed the smooth stone into Willow's hand. It was cold, so cold that it seemed to burn through flesh and bone and nerve. Willow trembled a little, holding it tightly, willing its power into herself.

"The child," said the gypsy. "You promised me that you would show me the child."

"I'll unlock the door." Her mind was working clearly and coolly. Once the key was in the woman's possession, her own safety would be threatened; she would have to be silenced while the child was being taken, and the suspiciously willing way in which the talisman had been handed over suggested that its owner intended to regain it very soon.

She stooped to the door that, a little way from the house, was buried in the snowy turf. The gypsy could not know that it led into the cellar used in the past for storing apples, but later abandoned because of its dampness. In the weeks following Caroline's birth, Willow had discovered the old cellar and appropriated the key with a vague idea that it might prove useful as a hiding place one day.

The door, weighted down with snow, was hard to pull back. The woman stood by, breathing heavily, making no attempt to help. The door fell back at last against the sloping grass, and a black shaft opened at their feet.

"It doesn't look like a way in," the woman said suspiciously.

"The ladder leads into the cellar. There's a connecting passage."

The gypsy approached, stooping to see. For an instant the thought flashed across Willow's mind—What if she spoke the truth? What if she really came by coach and wishes only to see her son's child for a few moments? What if she doesn't intend to murder me and take back the amulet after all?—a brief flash only and then her small, strong hands thrust themselves into the small of the gypsy's back and the tall, gaunt figure pitched headfirst into the sloping darkness. She was never sure afterward if the gypsy had cried out. What she did hear was the splintering of rotten wood as the disused ladder gave way, and the sharp crack as skull and stone banged together.

"Sarah? Are you there, Sarah?" She whispered softly down into the darkness, but could hear nothing. There was but a vague, silent shape below in the little stone-lined cellar.

"I suppose you're dead," she said, sitting back on her heels and tugging again at the door. People, she decided, die very easily. Of course, the woman had drunk quite a lot of the whisky.

The door locked again, she pushed handfuls of snow back over against it and rose to her feet. The moon was in full view again and she could see their footprints in the snow. She had forgotten about the footprints.

The black stone was still clenched in her fist. She held it up to the moonlight, and saw that what had been fire in its depths that afternoon was now a greenish glow deep in its heart. She turned it over and the green became silver and in the silver there were curling shapes of black, as if a hundred tiny snakes writhed and coiled in the empty air.

"Lilith," she said aloud. "Lilith of the dark side of the moon! Don't let them find the footsteps! Don't let anyone come seeking the gypsy! Lilith?"

Another nighthawk spread its dark shadow across the moon and a wind moaned softly, as if some black-veiled woman roused from a century's sleep.

Willow remounted her pony and felt the sharp sting of hail against her cheek. The wind was all about her, tugging at her hood, stirring up waves of powdery snow around the hoofs of the animal. The snow shifted like sand before the tide. The hail had thickened and softened into flakes, falling ever faster. By dawn not a print would remain.

"You're covered with snow and wet through!" Eliza cried as the girl shook off the clinging wetness at the cottage door.

"There was nobody at the manor," Willow said,

spreading her cloak over a chair. "I was almost there when I remembered Miss Browning was going to sup with Mr. Penn this evening. I can't think how I came to forget."

"It was a kind thought," Aunt Eliza said. "It would be very pleasant if you were to take an interest in little Caroline."

"Because we are both bastards?"

"Because you both have no father," Eliza said with faint reproach. "And Mair will not allow either of you to mix with Nathan or Joan."

"So the outcasts must get together? Oh, don't purse up your mouth like that, Auntie dear! I was only funning! Perhaps I should take an interest in little Caroline." Her small, cold hand closed over the black stone in her pocket.

"Shall we stay up to let in the New Year?" Eliza changed the subject, patting the cushion at her feet.

The girl had a strange, exalted look on her face and her hair, dripping over her thin shoulders had a greenish tinge, as if she had risen up through water. "If you wish." Willow spoke in her usual gentle tone but, ignoring her aunt's gesture, went over to the window, breathing hard on the cold glass, narrowing her eyes to better see the storm.

"You will be seventeen on your next birthday," Aunt Eliza said. "You'll be a young lady, Willow. Very soon you'll have to be thinking what you want to do with your life. This cottage will be yours when I die, you know. The cottage and the bit of money I've saved from my allowance."

"You're not going to die, are you?" Willow asked, half-turning from the window. Her eyes were anxious.

"No. I've every intention of living until I'm a hundred," Eliza said tranquilly. "But I don't want you to be worried, child. I want you to know that you'll always have a home and the means to live."

"I don't worry," Willow said calmly, turning again to the window. "I never worry about things like that. And I don't want to be a young lady, either. I want to go on as . . . we've always done."

"Well, I've reared you as best I could," Eliza said philosophically. "The rest is up to you. Your mother had a lot of character, you know. She was a fine wench, was Huldah Clegg. You have her blood in you."

"And Falcon blood, too," Willow said softly. "I have Falcon blood, Aunt dear, and the mark on my thigh."

"I ought never to have told you those old tales." Eliza winced as she shifted her leg into a more comfortable position. "But you wanted to know all about the family, and you had the right, being part of it."

"Yes, Aunt." She spoke gently still, but the black stone burned its icy fire into her palm.

Chapter 8

"Did you know that in the sunlight your hair has a golden glint?" Guto Evans asked.

"You're teasing me," Mair said primly, but her eyes were smiling. It was pleasant to be teased as if she were a girl again, pleasant to be told she was desirable—not, she reminded herself firmly, that she would ever do anything that even savored of unfaithfulness —but James was so busy and the doctor so attractive, with the flash of gypsy under his sensible professional manner. Imperceptibly she leaned a little closer, the full curve of her bosom swelling under the emerald silk of her dress.

They were in the drawing room, and May sunshine patterned the floor. Around them the old ornaments of ivory and silver twinkled at their reflections in the narrow, gilt-edged mirrors, and through the long windows stole the pale, fugitive scent of honeysuckle.

"You have a beautiful home," the doctor said, as if he picked up her thought and sealed it with his own approval.

"A veritable Eden," she said drily.

"Then there's a snake?" He raised black brows enquiringly.

"Four of them," she said sourly. "That wretchd governess, who had to go and get herself raped—"

"I had word that the gypsies privately hanged the man responsible."

"Which is of little comfort to me when the girl lives at the manor house still with her bastard child for company! And James insists that Nathan and Joan ride over to her for their lessons."

"And the other snakes are old Miss Falcon and the Clegg girl, I suppose?"

"My husband's precious Aunt Eliza and his bastard niece! If James had his way they'd live here at the big house, but I'd not allow that. His aunt's as mad as a hatter, anyway. Straw hat and breeches is her usual outfit, and she's sixty-five if she's a day! As for the Clegg girl!"

"You don't like her, either." His voice was amused.

"She . . . frightens me," Mair said, and for an instant her high color faded, as if some hand had reached out to wipe it away.

"Surely not! She's scarcely more than a child," he protested.

"Willow Clegg was never a child," Mair said. "Even when she was tiny there was a strangeness about her. A queer, empty look in her eyes. It makes me uneasy."

"You take her too seriously," he said gently.

"Perhaps. If only James were not so fond of her! Did you know that he is giving a party for her for her seventeenth birthday?"

"No, I didn't."

"You'll get your invitation in a day or two," she told him. "God knows what gave him the idea, but he has got it into his head that we ought to give Willow a party, some kind of celebration to mark the fact that she's now a young lady. In this house, if you please! He actually told me that if I refused to hold it here he would invite everybody to the manor and ask Miss Browning to act as hostess. You may imagine the scandal that would cause."

"Yes, indeed." He regarded her thoughtfully, admiring her style of beauty, but admitting to himself that she was neither clever nor subtle. It mattered little, for he preferred uncomplicated women, and under her ladylike exterior he sensed she was as passionate as a young animal.

"So who will come to this party?" he enquired.

"You and the Vicar and the Fiskes and the Stones." She ticked them off drearily on her fingers. "And Miss Browning and Aunt Eliza."

"And the girl."

"And Willow," she agreed. "I told James that giving a party for her would be like acknowledging her as a member of the family, and he told me that she was, after all, his brother's child, and that I ought to pity the girl."

"Perhaps he hopes to find a husband for her," he suggested.

"If that's the case, then I pity the poor man," Mair said fervently. "She has no love in her, I'll swear, and no man can exist with too little love."

Or too much, the doctor thought, and wondered if the master of *Kingsmead*'s concern for his dependents represented an attempt to break free of his wife's suffocating affection.

It would, he decided, his eyes straying again to the tempting roundness under the emerald silk, certainly be an interesting occasion. As a student of human nature he was looking forward to it.

His interest had not diminished when he sat, one
week later, at the long trestle table in the great hall.
It was, after all, a smaller company than had been
envisaged, the Fiskes and Stones having sent polite,
unconvincing regrets. The doctor sat, therefore, with
Aunt Eliza on his left and an excited and talkative
Joan on his right. She had been allowed to stay up—
over her mother's protests, he supposed—and was
chattering freely, her brown curls swinging at each
side of her flushed face. A normal, uncomplicated
child, the doctor thought, very like her brother. Nathan would be going away to school in the autumn;
meanwhile, he sat serenely blue-eyed and cheerful,
eating heartily and apparently oblivious to the cross-
currents of feeling raging about his head. The others,
with the possible exception of the Vicar, who sat
further down the table, were displaying a kind of
genteel ferocity, as if they would all have infinitely
preferred to have been tearing at one another instead
of the meat.

Eliza, resplendent in a figured brocade sacque gown
and a turban ornamented with pink and purple
plumes, seemed determined to establish once and for
all that her youthful charge had as much right to be
there as any of the family.

"I can remember your father, Willow, as clearly as
if it were yesterday. Sitting there, telling us of a
horse he'd just broken or some scheme he had afoot.
Don't you remember, James?"

James nodded, his eyes clouding. He had loved his
twin brother and never ceased to regret his death at
Trafalgar, even though that death had brought him
peerage and estate. But mention of Fairfax brought
with it the memory of Huldah Clegg whom he had
loved, whom Fairfax had seduced.

That love had waned into no more than a bitter-sweet nostalgia that occasionally disturbed his dreams. Since his marriage there had been no other woman in his life except Mair. She had proved an excellent wife and mother, though her possessiveness sometimes irked him. She was looking her best this evening in a gown of maroon and white, with a necklace of flat golden links. Her unruly hair was pulled into an elaborate chignon in which amethysts gleamed. He smiled at her and was rewarded with a fleeting, resentful stare.

It was a great pity that she could not bring herself to be more cordial to poor little Willow. It was as much as she could do to speak civilly to Aunt Eliza. He sighed inwardly, and offered Felice Browning a bread roll.

Felice had never felt more miserable in her life, not even when she was expecting her child and had to face the pity and contempt of the villagers. Time had dulled that horror, though the experience had left its mark on her. Youth and gaiety had fled from her step and her smile, and she shrank a little from even the casual touch of a man. Since Caroline's birth she had not entered *Kingsmead*, and to pass again under its roof had induced in her a shivering nervousness. Lord James had been very kind, insisting that Nathan and Joan come over to the manor for their lessons, bringing small gifts for the baby. If she sometimes wondered how it might have been if she had not set out for the little church that evening, she crushed down the thought, reminding herself that she was more fortunate than many a young girl in the same position, and that Lord James had been incredibly kind.

"You look tired, Miss Browning," Lady Mair said,

leaning forward slightly with her heavy brows raised.

Immediately Felice was conscious of her cheap, pink sateen dress and her lack of jewellery. She had tried to brighten and enrich her outfit with posies of little ribbon flowers in shades of blue and lilac and green, but the effect seemed faintly garish now.

"I am perfectly well, Lady Mair," she said stiffly.

"And the child?"

"Her name is Caroline," Aunt Eliza put in loudly. "Don't pretend not to remember it."

"Caroline is very well, too," Felice said, increasingly uncomfortable.

"Such a pretty little thing!" the Vicar said, leaping into the breach. "I shall be happy to instruct her when she is of age."

"Filling her poor little head with church-going," Aunt Eliza said quite loudly. "I had my fill of worship when I was a child, thank you very much!"

"Some of us are privileged to be unconventional," Mair said.

"Or old enough to say what they please, eh, Dr. Evans?" Aunt Eliza nudged him painfully in the ribs.

"I'm sure you have always said exactly what you please, Miss Falcon," he returned smoothly.

"Not always. When I was a girl I can tell you there was only one person in this house whose opinion was ever considered important, and that was my father."

"I've heard many tales of old Lord Falcon's strong personality," Mr. Penn ventured timidly.

"He was a tyrant," Eliza said flatly, "but I'll grant you he had a strong personality. Miss Browning, you must take no heed of what my nephew's wife says. You look very charming and I hear nothing but good reports of your little girl. If Caroline grows up to do you the credit that Willow does me, then you will have nothing of which to complain."

Eyes turned toward Willow, who sat next to her uncle, her light hair brushed smoothly over her shoulders, her eyelids downcast.

Her gown, which she had chosen herself, was of white gauze, pleated high under her small bust and falling sheer to her ankles. The only decoration on the dress was a sash of purple velvet, its ends fashioned like the head and tail of a snake, the eyes embroidered in crystal, the tongue a flick of emerald silk. The dress, thought Guto Evans, was a cunning mixture of the innocent and the subtle. It also made the other women look overdressed. Yet the girl did not attract him. She was too slim and small, and there was something feline in her slanted eyes and the way in which her small tongue stole out and licked her curving lips.

"When I am older," Joan piped up, "may I stop going to church, too?"

"Indeed you may not," her mother said sharply. "Sit up properly and hold your tongue. Mr. Penn, I must apologize for Joan. I fear in the excitement of being allowed to stay up she has forgotten her manners."

"I am not excited!" Joan said indignantly.

"Hush, my pet." James gave her an indulgent shake of the head. "Now, my dear niece, I do think that the time has come for us all to drink a toast to you. Ladies and gentlemen, will you rise and wish with me all health and happiness to Willow on the happy occasion of her seventeenth birthday!"

The toast was drunk, Mair barely touching her lips to her glass. Willow, her lashes still veiling her eyes, said in her sweetly precise voice, "May I thank you all for coming, and may I thank you, dear uncle, for giving this party for me? Lady Mair, too, of course. I can see you have both gone to a great deal of trouble for me, and it is very pleasant to be invited to *Kingsmead*."

Very clever, thought the doctor leaning back in his chair and enjoying the nearly imperceptible emphasis Willow had given the word *"invited."* The minx had carefully separated Lord and Lady Falcon and presented herself as the innocent recipient of belated charity.

Mair was biting her lip with annoyance, but suddenly Nathan was staring at his cousin as if he had never seen a girl before. He was tall for his age, with long legs and broad shoulders and a merry, pleasant expression on his frank face.

Willow raised her lashes and gazed back at him for a few seconds, wistfully and gently.

Why, the girl is only three years older than he is, and in a short time that will count for nothing, the doctor thought. He wondered if Mair had noticed, but she was still staring at her husband, who, avoiding her glance, poured more wine for Miss Browning. The governess looked very pale. Her fingers, clutching the fragile stem of the glass, trembled as his broad hand hovered above with the decanter.

"It doesn't seem seventeen years since you were born, my dear." James, setting the decanter in its place, turned again to Willow.

"We are all getting old," Mr. Penn said.

"Speak for yourself!" Eliza ordered. "I'm feeling remarkably frisky tonight. James, may I trouble you for some more of that excellent wine? And do permit Joan to leave the table. She is fidgeting quite abominably."

"May I show Willow round the house?" Joan demanded, wriggling to her feet.

"There is no need to embark on a conducted tour," Mair began.

"But the family portraits," Nathan said. "You would like to see the family portraits, wouldn't you, cousin?" His eyes, fixed on Willow's small face, were eager.

"Yes, indeed," Willow said gently.

"There's a card table set out in the drawing room," Mair said.

"Then we'll leave the young ones to look at the portraits, shall we?" James helped Mair to her feet. He wore the slightly anxious expression of a husband who knows he has offended his wife and is not certain how to make amends.

Mair shook her arm free with a little impatient gesture and walked ahead of them into the drawing room.

"Miss Browning, do you care for whist or faro?" James asked, his face reddening slightly as he turned to her.

"I use to play both sometimes with my father." Her hand, resting on his proferred arm, still trembled, and the glance of her blue eyes were timidly imploring.

She's in love with him, Guto Evans thought. Poor, pretty creature! She hasn't a chance of landing her catch, for he's the very model of a faithful husband— not that Mair would ever believe it were it put to the test.

"Is it true," Mr. Penn was asking, "that one of the portraits was painted by your father, Lady Mair?"

"The family group." It was Eliza who answered. "Geraint Price, a Welshman, was the artist. He rode into Marie Regina looking for a patron and found my little sister, Apple. They eloped, you know, as did my other sister, Helen. In our family, with my father around, it was necessary to elope if you were female and craved a husband."

"As you never did?" the doctor enquired.

"I never had much use for males save as stallions," Eliza said cheerfully. "I saw too much of the way my father treated my mother."

"I loved grandfather," James said with a tinge of reproach.

"You love everybody," Eliza said. "Even as a little boy you loved everybody."

"And Lady Mair was not born at *Kingsmead* then?"

"I was born in Wales," Mair said. "My mother had a little farm there that an old aunt had willed to her. She and my father worked it together. He never did make his name as an artist."

"But they were happy? My sister and her artist were happy?"

"Yes, yes, they were happy," Mair said slowly.

A memory of childhood had swept over her so vividly that the long room with its chandeliers and silk drapes faded. The living room at Saron had served also as a kitchen. The fire had crackled on the hearth below the soup caldron, and in winter the snow had crept down from the high peaks of Snowdonia and whitened the pasture. Her father had been dark and quiet, with dead dreams in his eyes, and her mother had been merry and red-haired.

"Saron was where the witch came from," she heard herself say. "The one who married her daughter into the Falcon's and laid the curse upon the family. She bore the devil's kiss on her thigh, my mother said."

"Apple bore the mark, too," said Aunt Eliza.

"As I do." There was challenge in Mair's brown eyes. "I too bear the mark."

"So does Willow," said Aunt Eliza. "It must be the first time that two Falcon women have borne the mark in one generation."

"But I know the words of the curse," Mair said. "My mother taught them to me just before she died."

"Then it is your duty to hand them on," said Eliza.

"To Willow Clegg? I'll hand them to nobody."

"If my nephew Fairfax had married Huldah Clegg, then Willow would have been a Falcon in law as well as in blood. She has the right to hear the words."

"Not from me. Never from me!"

"These old traditions," said the Vicar uncomfortably, "are so interesting."

"Joan and Nathan—" Aunt Eliza cocked an enquiring eyebrow.

"Have no mark," Mair said tensely. "No shadow touches them. And the words die with me."

Aunt Eliza regarded her steadily and then nodded slowly. "It will probably be for the best," she said. "But Willow has the right to be considered part of the family."

"James has always—"

"Not James. You!"

"Aunt, these are private matters and our guests are waiting to play cards," James said.

"I hope I shall always do my duty," Mair said coldly. "My husband has several dependents, and devotes time and money to them all."

"If you are referring to me," Felice Browning said in a shrill, nervous voice, "I do everything in my power to repay milord's generosity to me. Truly I do!" Her hands twining in the cheap sateen of her gown, she was blinking rapidly to hold back tears.

"I always feel," said Mr. Penn desperately, "that charity is the most beautiful word in the language."

"Do you indeed?" said Eliza. "How extraordinary!"

"I don't feel well," Joan said loudly from the door-way.

"You've eaten too much, my pet," James said.

"No more than I usually do," Joan complained. "But my head hurts and I feel shivery all over."

"Let me feel your head," Mair said, crossing to her daughter and bending down. Her voice, as she looked up, was sharp with alarm. "Her forehead is burning, James!"

"Let me see." Guto Evans was the professional man now, and not the cynically amused guest.

"It's probably a spring fever," Eliza said. "Children are often subject to them."

"Joan has never ailed in her life," Mair said.

"It's probably no more than a chill," the doctor agreed, but a frown lingered on his brow.

"What else could it be?" James asked.

"Nothing. Probably nothing at all."

"I heard there were two cases of smallpox over in Maidstone a few days ago," Mr. Penn ventured.

"Smallpox? Is that true?" James asked urgently.

"I'm afraid it is," the doctor said reluctantly. "I didn't want to mention it."

"Smallpox." Mair had backed a step, her eyes dilat-ing. "Oh, dear Lord, not smallpox."

"There's no need to alarm the child," Guto said in warning. "This is probably no more than a chill, but you'd better get her up to bed. Brew up a tisane, if you like. It won't do much good, but it won't do any harm, either."

"But if it is smallpox—" Eliza began. Under the nodding plumes of the turban her face was pinched and old.

"Surely you had the children vaccinated against smallpox," the doctor protested.

"I don't believe in these new-fangled treatments," Eliza said.

"Neither does James," Mair said shortly.

"Hardly new-fangled!" Guto protested. "It's more than twenty years since Jenner discovered the prevention. I could vaccinate her now if you like, as a precaution."

"There's no need. It's a slight fever, no more." James stooped and picked up Joan, smoothing down her ruffled curls.

"I must call Willow. Best for her to get home at once," Eliza said.

"Nathan!" James, still holding Joan, called through the doorway. "Nathan, bring your cousin downstairs. Joan is not well, and the party is ending."

In the gallery above the great hall, Nathan stared at Willow. "Joan is never ill," he said. "I suppose she ate too much at dinner."

"Little girls often eat too much," Willow said calmly. "Is this the witch-girl? Is this Catrin?"

"They say her mother was the one who made the curse and planted the luck tree outside the courtyard," Nathan said.

"I have her face," Willow said, looking up at the portrait.

"But her hair is red," said Nathan, "and her eyes are yellow. Yellow like a cat's eyes."

"And my hair is fair." She drew a strand of it through her fingers and slanted a smile at him.

"And your eyes are . . . like water," Nathan said. "I can't see the color of them."

"They change," Willow said. "It depends on my

mood, on the people I'm with. Your eyes are blue, very blue."

"Are they?" Nathan's face was crimson, but his hand stole out and clasped her thin fingers. From downstairs Eliza's voice sounded, "Willow! Willow, do hurry now! Joan is not well and we must go home."

Chapter 9

"If you had allowed me to have the children vaccinated, this would never have happened," Mair said.

"My dear, there are dangers inherent in all these new-fangled treatments," James protested.

"New-fangled! You heard Dr. Evans say that it has been possible to insure against the disease for more than twenty years."

"Dr. Evans is an intelligent young man, I've no doubt," James said wryly, "but he is inexperienced. A few months in a London hospital and he imagines he knows how to solve every problem under the sun."

"You give him no credit," she said resentfully. "You never have tried to help him to establish his practice here. The village needs a doctor of its own. Otherwise all the people are dependent upon stupid old women who can do nothing but what their grandmothers did."

"Often very effectively."

"And that doesn't help Joan." She came nearer, clutching at his sleeve, her eyes dark and sleep-starved. "James, our daughter has smallpox! Does that mean nothing to you?"

"It means everything to me," he said in reproach. "Joan is my treasure and I will not—cannot—contemplate anything happening to her."

"It *has* happened! She is very sick. Dr. Evans says—"

"I intend to ride to Maidstone and bring back a doctor from there—"

"Who will tell you exactly the same thing! Smallpox is smallpox. And there are five more cases in Maidstone since last week."

"She will be better when the eruptions break out."

"Little you know about it!" she said scornfully. "You have not sat up with her night after night since she fell sick."

"Because you will not allow me in the room."

"I could not risk your falling sick," she said with a catch in her voice. "If anything happened to you I would die, too."

"At least let Eliza help you with the nursing," he pleaded. "She has begged to come over and help."

"Let her stay in the Dower Cottage where she belongs!" Mair snapped. "There was never any sickness until she and Willow Clegg came here."

"You're tired and overwrought." He patted her shoulder consolingly.

"I am neither!" she said defiantly. "I can continue indefinitely, I promise you."

"But there must be something I can do," he said, helplessly.

"Ride down to the village and enquire if there are any more cases of the sickness," she said.

"We would have heard—"

"Go anyway! Anything is better than having you wander about here getting under my feet."

"I'll take Nathan—" he began.

"Nathan is over at the manor," she reminded him, "having a French lesson. Dr. Evans thought it better for him to continue as normally as possible, but not to go into the village. You are not going to go against the doctor's advice, I hope."

"Not if you don't wish it," he said defeated.

"And you won't stay away long?" Having urged him to go, some irrational impulse made her cling to him again. Her vibrant, dark hair was dull and uncombed, and there were patches of sweat under her arms. In the bright sunlight she looked every minute of her thirty-six years. He held her closely for a moment, wishing desperately that she would allow him to help her. Then she disengaged herself gently and plodded slowly up the stairs toward the bedroom where Joan lay, scarlet-cheeked and dryly burning, recognizing no one.

For James it was—though it shamed him to admit the fact—a relief to mount his horse and ride out across the courtyard into the open. Sickness had a depressing effect upon him at the best of times, and such a disease as smallpox with all its attendant horrors stifled the hope in his heart. Yet it was unthinkable that his smiling, uncomplicated daughter should die. Neither Nathan nor Joan had ever caused him the faintest anxiety.

He had ridden across the bridge before he noticed Willow sitting on the parapet, clad in her favorite green, her feet dangling over the edge.

"Are you looking for Nathan?" she enquired, without preliminary greetings.

"He's at the manor house, isn't he?"

"He came over to the cottage," she said. "Aunt Eliza is brewing a tisane to keep any infection at bay. If you're going into the village you won't find the doctor there. He had to ride over to Maidstone to get some fresh supplies, and he won't be back until this evening. Is Cousin Joan better?"

"She's no worse," he said briefly, pain striking him. "And you are quite well?"

"I never ail, Uncle dear." She bestowed upon him her quick, slanting smile.

"Then what are you doing here?" he asked curiously.

"Dreaming and wishing," she said. "Wishing and dreaming, Uncle dear."

"When this is over, we will have to think about finding you a husband," he said. "You know, don't you, that you may count upon a dowry from me?"

"You're always generous," she said softly.

"Long ago I loved your mother very much," he said, "and for her sake, and for my brother's sake, I'll not see you lonely or in want."

"You're very generous," she said again. "Very generous, indeed."

"Willow! Willow, are you up there?" Nathan's brown head popped up above the level of the road as he climbed up the narrow bridle path. His face clouded as he saw his father, and he said in quick anxiety, "Joan isn't worse, is she?"

"No, no. Your mother's with her. Why aren't you at your lessons?"

"Miss Browning didn't feel very well, so she sent me off," Nathan explained. "I met Willow down by the river and she asked me if I'd like to go and visit Aunt Eliza. It is all right, isn't it?"

"Miss Browning sick?" James disregarded the latter part of his son's speech. "What's wrong with her?"

"Her head aches and she feels dizzy." Nathan turned again to Willow saying, "Aunt Eliza wants you to come back to the cottage for something to eat. She says you had no breakfast at all."

"I never do eat much, cousin dear." But she slid down from the parapet and took the boy's outstretched hand.

"I'll ride over to the manor and see if Miss Browning is feeling better," James decided. "Or does Aunt Eliza intend to go?"

"Miss Browning told me not to say anything to Aunt Eliza. She doesn't want to make a fuss," Nathan said.

"But you told Willow."

"People," said Willow, "tell me things."

"If Aunt Eliza has no objection, you'd better stay at the cottage until suppertime," James said to Nathan. "*Kingsmead* is cheerless enough, God knows! Ride back at suppertime." He was impatient to be at the manor, to see for himself that Miss Browning's indisposition was no more than trifling. He felt a deep sense of responsibility toward the delicate young woman who had been so cruelly abused and had borne her child with such courage. If only Mair were more sympathetic! He sighed, wishing that he understood women better.

The manor had about it an air of solitariness. He dismounted and pushed through the front door which was left ajar, the deaf servant maid being unable to hear the jangling of the bell that announced visitors.

The hall, more modestly proportioned than the hall at *Kingsmead*, stretched ahead, quiet and sunlit, doors on the left and right leading to parlor and kitchen, He stood, his eyes moving slowly from the woven tapestries which graced the walls to the staircase that reached up to the rooms above.

He had chosen the furnishings for the manor in the days when he was in love with Huldah Clegg. Her face was still clear in his mind, the skin honey-tanned, the blunt nose freckled. The feelings he had once for her were muted now, lost in the deeper love he had for his wife.

He sighed again and raised his voice, calling, "Miss Browning! Are you there, Miss Browning?" A wail sounded from upstairs, the wail of a young child.

James took the stairs two at a time and ran into the larger of the two bedrooms. The tiny room between them had been fitted up as a sewing-room, and the corner of a half-finished tapestry was visible through the open door.

In the bedroom the tiny, black-haired girl bounced indignantly on the feather mattress of her crib. Her face was scarlet and streaked with tears, and her shrill little voice rose unavailingly. "Wake up, Mamma! Wake up! Caro's sleeped now. Want to get up! *Marima!*"

"Miss Browning?" James went over to the larger bed and leaned over the slim figure.

"I feel so dizzy," she said painfully through cracked lips. "I feel so dizzy and my head aches. Milord, my head aches so badly!"

"I'll bring you some water." He poured some from the ewer into a glass and brought it to her, putting his arm behind her shoulders so that she could drink with more ease.

"I sent Nathan to Aunt Eliza," she said. "I've been lying down since, but Caro wants her dinner."

"Where's the maid?" he demanded.

"Gone back to the village. I sent her back to her

mother for a few days. I don't want her to get sick, too. Caro needs some dinner."

"I'll give her some," he promised hastily.

The little girl had stopped crying and clung round his neck as he picked her up. She knew James well, for he was the only man who came regularly to the manor, apart from Nathan, who in her eyes was already grown up, and whom she adored.

In the kitchen he found some apple pie and some buttermilk, and sat the child on his knee as she ate. She was a dainty creature, her eyes china-blue, her hair clustering about her head in tight ringlets that sprang back into place when he pulled them.

"Will you play in the garden, chuck? Play like a good girl and not run away?" he enquired as she wriggled down.

"Caro's sticky," she informed him. He found a damp cloth and scraped traces of sugared apple from the pink lips. There was no sign in the little face turned up to him of her brutal begetting. Everything about her sang an innocent sweetness.

He drew his forefinger down the side of her small nose and said, "Now, will you play like a good girl, while I take care of Mamma?"

"With my dolly," she nodded, and trotted across to the windowseat where a rag doll was sprawled with its legs in the air.

He left the dishes on the table and hurried back upstairs. Felice seemed to be asleep, but she muttered uneasily, and when he put his hand on her burning forehead she jerked sharply and cried out.

"Miss Browning, shall I ride to the cottage and bring Aunt Eliza back?" he asked.

She evidently heard him, for she clutched at his arm, exclaiming, "No! Oh, no, please!"

"But Aunt Eliza came when your child was born," he said, puzzled.

"The infection," she said. "I don't want her to catch the infection." It was not the whole truth, but she could not tell him that if Eliza came, then Willow would probably come, too, and there was something about Willow that made her feel cold and sick. She sometimes remembered the first afternoon when she had arrived at *Kingsmead* and seen the green figure flitting elf-like among the trees. That seemed so long ago, and since then her whole life had changed. Her mind still shuddered away from that evening in the deer park when the thick-set man had sprang upon her. But the gypsy had only been a part of the unhappiness she had known since she had first seen Willow Clegg.

"Stay with me, milord," she begged. "Please stay, milord." Her hand was hot and dry. Tiny red pustules were erupting about her hairline and under the lobes of her ears. "Please stay," she said again, and began to cry weakly.

James stared down at her in an agony of indecision. If he left her to go for help, there was no telling what she might take it into her fevered brain to do. And Aunt Eliza was no longer young. He had heard somewhere that the old and the young were susceptible to the disease. He could have ridden to the village, but there were few who were willing to nurse a case of smallpox.

He recalled unwillingly the evening that she had ridden to the little church. If he had gone with her she would never have been attacked. The feeling of responsibility that was part of his nature rose up in him strongly.

"I'll stay with you," he said at last. When dusk came,

Nathan might come to the manor house. Then he could send the boy into the village to find out if Dr. Evans had returned from Maidstone. Meanwhile, the girl tossed and muttered in a half-delirium, and needed to be sponged down. As he poured water into a basin he glanced out of the window and saw Caro sitting on the grass with the rag doll in her arms. He would have to remember to give the child some supper and move her crib into the other room. She was such a good little thing!

The long sunlit afternoon drained into twilight. James went down to bring in Caro and found her putting her doll to bed on a mass of leaves she had pulled. She was crooning as she patted the greenery into place and he looked at her with pleasure, wishing that the world was full of children.

She ate her supper daintily, without asking to see her mother, and allowed him to take off her dress and shoes and stockings. There was a clean nightgown in the linen chest. He put it on her and tucked her into the crib. She wrinkled her nose at the room and said, "Mary sleeps here. Not Caro."

"Mary has gone away for a little while," he coaxed. "Will Caro stay here just for tonight?"

She nodded and said on a hinting note, "Mamma tells stories."

"Uncle James will tell stories tomorrow," he promised. "Will you go to sleep now, like a good girl?"

"Caro wants a light," she said. "Caro wants a light, in case the bogey comes."

"There are no such things, my darling," he assured her.

"Two, on a horse," she said solemnly. "Caro was on the windowseat, and it was dark. Two on a horse, and one fell into the ground. Caro seed them."

"Caro had a nightmare," he said. "But I'll leave the candle, if you promise not to touch it."

He kissed her again, tucked the blankets about her, and went out, shaking his head slightly, remembering how as a child he himself had often woken in a cold sweat, struggling out of some boyish terror. The imagination of a child was a delicate and mysterious thing.

Felice still lay in a troubled, tossing sleep. Her face was covered with the virulent spots and so were her hands. She muttered incoherently, and once she said quite clearly, "But I never meant to love him." Some young man, he supposed, on whom she had fixed her fancy before the deaths of her parents had forced her to seek a situation as governess. And now it was highly unlikely that any man would ever want to marry her.

In pity he put his arms about her, saying, "I'm here now, my dear." And evidently she mistook him for someone else, for she put her arms round his neck and held on tightly, as if she were Caro.

He sat on the edge of the bed, holding her, murmuring to her when she stirred; as the moon rayed out its first light, he felt the cool, health-bringing sweat break out, drenching her thin cotton shift.

The attack was evidently a light one. He eased her back onto the pillows and stretched his cramped limbs. She was breathing easily now, her blue eyes closed. He bent over her, saying clearly, "You will be better soon. I'm going to get Aunt Eliza now."

The danger of infection was surely past, and it was time he was getting home before Mair began to fret. He pulled the covers around her shoulders and tiptoed across the landing to the other room where Caro slept, one thumb in her mouth, the other hand curved about her rag doll.

The manor house was quiet, the drive a curving ribbon of stillness in the moonlight. He rode swiftly, glad of the cool breeze on his face after the long hours in the stuffy bedroom. He clattered over the bridge and down the bridle path towards the clearing where the Dower Cottage stood. There was a light in one of the lower windows, and Willow came around the side of the house as he drew rein.

For an instant she stood in the shaft of light flung across the moss, and then she moved toward him, becoming part of the moonlight again. "Is anything wrong, Uncle dear?" she enquired.

"Miss Browning is sick of the smallpox," he told her, "but it's only a light attack, I think, and she's over the worst of it."

"Poor Miss Browning! How dreadful to be ill!" she exclaimed softly.

"James, is that you out there?" Eliza demanded, flinging open the door.

"I've been over at the manor all afternoon," he told her. "Miss Browning is ill."

"Not the pox?"

"A light attack, I think, but I was afraid to leave her until now. Can you ride over to take care of her, Aunt Eliza?"

"I can take care of her," Willow said.

"Don't be foolish, child," Eliza said. "You cannot risk the danger of infection!"

"I doubt if there is much risk of that," James assured her. "But you have more experience of nursing, Aunt."

"I'll saddle up and be on my way," she said promptly. "Willow, you'd best stay here. Come over in the morning to see if there's anything I need. James, will you ask Dr. Evans to call at the manor as soon as possible? He'll be back from Maidstone by tomorrow, I suppose. Willow, be sure to damp down the fire and lock the door. Don't spend half the night gazing at the moon! I sent Nathan home about an hour since. Is Caro alright?"

"She's fine. I put her to bed in the maid's room. Fast asleep when I looked in on her."

But Eliza was already heading toward the lean-to housing the horses, and Willow had again vanished into the woods. Left alone, and feeling helplessly tired, Lord James Falcon pulled himself into the saddle and turned his horse to home.

He watched amused as his aunt bustled in and out, collecting bags and shawls. Willow stood very still, her eyes moving between them, her hair a pale waterfall.

"You'd best ride home and see how Joan does," Aunt Eliza said, emerging with a colored scarf tied over her straw hat and an ulster pulled around her shoulders.

"We hope she'll soon be quite well again," Willow breathed.

He sketched a salute to them both and rode out of the clearing up to the main road again. Nathan had probably sneaked up to his room, to avoid having to tell his mother that he had visited the cottage. James hoped that Mair had succeeded in getting some rest. If she insisted on continuing without help she would be completely exhausted.

He quickened pace as he rode through the open gateway of *Kingsmead*. There were lights shining out from the unshuttered windows, and the front door was unbolted. He pushed it open and stood on the threshold, aware of the chill that came from the untended fire and from something else, something indefinable but unmistakable.

Mair was coming down the stairs, moving slowly

and draggingly, as if she were an old woman. He went forward to meet her, his hand stretched out toward her, and heard his own voice, louder and heartier than usual. "I'm sorry to have been such a long time, my dear. Miss Browning was taken sick and I had to stay with her. Aunt Eliza has ridden over to the manor now. My dear—"

"Joan is dead," she said in a flat, dull voice from which all emotion had fled. "An hour ago. Joan died an hour ago. Quite suddenly, you know. Quite suddenly."

"But you should have—if you had sent for me—" He was stammering, guilt and grief flooding him. "If you had sent for me!"

"Dr. Evans came," she said, and her heavy eyes accused him. "He came from Maidstone with physic for Joan. Straight here without stopping to change his clothes or have a meal. But she couldn't swallow anything. And she died. She died."

"My dear, my dear." Sobs tore at his throat and his eyes filled with tears.

"You should have come home earlier," she said in the same cold, dry voice.

"I was coming," he said miserably, "but I was delayed at the manor."

"Yes. You were at the manor," she agreed, and turning began to mount the stairs again without looking back.

Chapter 10

Guto Evans leaned back and crossed his arms under
his head. Through half-closed eyes he watched Mair
as she pinned up her hair again. It was soothing to
watch the slow, languid movements of her arms, to see
the creamy skin of her breasts as they swelled over
her tight chemise. Her waist and hips were thickening,
but she had magnificent shoulders and hair, and in
the aftermath of love her lashes lay heavy above her
cheekbones.

"I ought not to come here so often," she remarked
to her reflection in the glass. "People will begin to
notice."

"You have the right to visit your doctor, especially
when he is your tenant," he said.

"Wasn't it fortunate that James bought me this
cottage as an anniversary present?" she said.

"Just in time for you to rent it to me."

"For a peppercorn rent." She laughed, displaying
her strong white teeth.

She had laughed a lot in the three months since
Joan's death. Sometimes she would laugh until the

tears rolled down her face, and then her eyes would grow hard again and her wide mouth would thin into a narrow line. Recently he had sensed a kind of desperation in the ardor with which she had responded to him.

Thinking of that now he said, "Is everything still bad at home? Are things no better?"

"They are worse." She wriggled into her gown, her face averted. "James spends his days in the fields, his evenings down at the cottage or up at the manor. He has not touched me since Joan died."

"Do you want him—to touch you?"

"I hate him!" she cried in sudden violence. "I shall never forgive him for leaving me on that day, for not coming home. As if a mere governess was as precious as his own child! And such a trifling attack it was! Why, she was up within the week, without a mark on her face to show that she had even had the pox."

"I was there," he reminded her.

"Yes, you were there." She came swiftly to the bed and knelt beside it. "I never shall forget that you were there, that you comforted me when my own husband was absent! And for that I will not forgive him, nor let him touch me again."

"You will drive him to the governess," he warned.

"Much I care! She is welcome to him," Mair said lightly, but she rose, brushing dust from her skirt, saying, "This place is a veritable disgrace! I think I shall have to get you a neat, respectable woman to clean the house."

"And find a stray ribbon or an earring? No thank you."

"They would be mine, I hope?"

"No other woman comes here," he said truthfully, and thought in a cool, detached manner, Why should

I invite any, or seek any, when you are here to serve my needs and satisfy my lusts?

He had, he considered, fallen upon pleasant paths in this small village, for though his practice remained small and many still regarded him with suspicion, his earnings were sufficient for his small needs and his mistress was rich and passionate. He smiled up at her, his narrow eyes sleepy, his mouth shaping into the parody of a kiss.

"I shall never forgive James," she said loudly.

"But Nathan is well?"

"And enjoying his school. I was afraid he might be homesick, but he seems glad to be with other boys." Her voice was wistful, for she had secretly hoped that Nathan would complain and beg to stay at home with her, but he had seemed eager to be gone, and for that she blamed James who had filled the boy's head with nonsense about boarding schools.

"I have to go," she said, tying on her hat and reaching for her cloak. "There are still duties for me at *Kingsmead*, you know. The preserves must be put up, and the meat jellied, and the apples stored for the winter. It's close on October now and there's a long winter ahead."

"But you'll come again soon?" His hand caught at her skirt, fondling her thigh.

"Yes, yes, of course." She looked down at him, aware that part of his attraction for her lay in the fact that he desired her, that he still found her an attractive woman. If James would only come to her, and beg her pardon, and make her weep in his arms, but after that meeting on the stairs he had avoided her, speaking on the rare occasions they met with a grave and distant courtesy. If only James would—she clamped down the thought and bent to kiss her lover who stretched, lazily content, like a lean and satisfied tom-cat.

In the street, as she climbed up to the seat of the pony trap, she saw Willow Clegg. Like herself the girl was clad in mourning, and the sight of the black garments and demure bonnet roused in Mair a cold anger.

"Does Aunt Eliza allow you to wander about dragging your skirts in the dust?" she asked sharply.

"I am going to see Dr. Evans," Willow said.

"You look healthy enough," Mair said.

"It's a social call," Willow said. "Like the call you have just made. It is permitted, is it not, for a young lady to pay a social call?"

"An unmarried girl should have a chaperone."

"But a married lady may visit whom she pleases?" Willow wrinkled her small nose and put her head on one side, enquiring, "And may an unmarried lady receive visitors? Miss Browning—"

"What of Miss Browning?"

"Why, nothing. I was only going to say that Miss Browning has no husband but she receives visitors. Uncle James—"

"Lord Falcon's activities are none of your concern," Mair snapped.

"But I am exceedingly interested," Willow said gently, "in everything the Falcons do. It must be lonely for you now that Nathan has gone."

"I am far too busy to give any heed to loneliness."

"Ah, yes, of course." The light eyes flicked to the upper window of the doctor's house.

"You had better pay your call," Mair said, gathering up the reins and clicking her tongue.

"I think I'll wait until I can find a chaperone," Willow said brightly, "or until I'm a married lady and can visit whom I please." She moved quickly as she spoke, clambering up to the pony trap.

"I didn't ask you to join me," Mair said tightly.

"I wish to ask a favor of you," Willow said, folding her hands together demurely.

"If there is anything you need surely Lord Falcon will provide it."

"He cannot provide this," Willow said. "Only you know the words."

"Words?"

"The words of the curse. You know the words of the curse. Aunt Eliza told me that your mother bore the mark as we do. She must have passed the words down to you. They are always passed down. I am a Falcon, too, I bear the mark, and I have a right to know those words."

"You have no rights!" Mair jerked the pony to a standstill and turned a furious face toward the younger girl. "You have no rights, Willow Clegg! Your mother was a slut who gave herself to the first man who smiled at her! And after she died there was nobody who would have the shame of rearing you, except Aunt Eliza, who has always been half-crazy! You have nothing, save what Lord Falcon allows you out of his charity!"

"So you will not tell me." Willow's voice was quiet, her face still. "Well, I will not beg. I begged you once, and you killed my dog."

"It was an accident! It was an accident!"

"Such a sad one," Willow said gently. "And isn't it strange how one accident can begin such a long period of ill luck? Poor Uncle Weston, to die so suddenly! And he wasn't so very old, was he? And then the smallpox came. And only poor Joan to die of it! Wasn't that sad?"

"I want you," Mair said, breathing with difficulty, "I want you to get out of this trap and go away, back to the cottage or . . . or your own part of the woods. But don't come near me or mine again. Don't ever come near me again."

Willow climbed down obediently. Her black skirts and bonnet made her look fragile and pathetic. In one small palm she clutched something tightly.

"Don't come near me again," Mair said, and lashed the pony into a gallop.

Willow stood still, watching the pony trap sway over the bridge. She watched until the curve of the road hid it from sight, and then she looked down at the gleaming black stone in her hand.

"I will have Uncle James make a ring out of you," she said in a low voice. "A beautiful black ring that shines under the moon. And the ring and the power will both be mine; mine so strongly that I won't need the words. I won't need anything." She slipped the stone into her pocket and began to descend the bridle path. The leaves were changing color and little heaps of them crunched beneath her feet.

"Willow! Why, I almost ran you down!" The exclamation came from James who pulled up his mount abruptly as he caught sight of her.

"I was in a daydream." She gave him a shy, upward glance.

"What were you daydreaming about?" he enquired.

"About poor little Joan," she said softly. "I went to the churchyard, just to say a little prayer, you know, and I thought how happy she always was when autumn came and she could scuffle all the leaves."

His face had changed, sadness invading his features. "You should not be wandering about in the churchyard," he said kindly. "A young girl should have more cheerful thoughts."

"I was on my way to see Dr. Evans," she explained. "Aunt Eliza wishes to ask him for supper, but I—I didn't call there."

"Why not?"

"He was—occupied," she hesitated. "I didn't like to intrude, and when Lady Mair came out—"

"Mair was there?"

"She came out and gave me such a fierce look, as if I was intruding, so I came away. She is not ill, is she?"

"Not to my knowledge," he said, frowning.

"Perhaps she was there to collect her rent," Willow suggested.

"The steward does that." He gave a slight shake of his head, as if he were conducting some interior argument, and said, "Perhaps she had other business to discuss."

"I suppose so," Willow agreed tranquilly. "Have you been to the cottage?"

"To see Aunt Eliza. I went into Maidstone to see my lawyer yesterday, to make certain provisions in my will."

"But you're not going to die, are you?" she asked in genuine agitation. "The smallpox is gone now!"

"I hope to live to be a century," he said smiling, "but I want to be sure that when I do pass away I leave my affairs in good order. *Kingsmead* is entailed and will pass to Nathan, as will the manor house, but there are Wittle Farm and Paget Place. They came into our family through marriage and I may leave them to whom I please, as Aunt Eliza may leave the cottage."

She nodded solemnly, thinking of the handsome dwellings in Maidstone that had come into the family nearly two hundred years before when the notorious

Regina Falcon had wed old Nathaniel Paget. It was a fine building, rented out from time to time, but remaining part of the Falcon estate.

"The Wittle property," James said, "is going to be yours, my dear."

"Mine?" She stared at him.

"You know that your mother was born on the farm? Your grandfather was bailiff to my grandfather. He was a fine man, was Samuel Clegg. I wish you could remember him, but he died when you were little, and I've not had the heart since to put another bailiff in."

"Because of my mother?"

"I once loved her very much," he said quietly, "and Wittle Farm shall go to her daughter; to you, my dear."

Willow was silent. She knew the Wittle farmstead well, for it lay beyond the monastery ruins at the other side of the hill. The house was a small, solidly built dwelling place enclosed within a cobbled yard. It had been closed up for years, though the land was still worked.

"You're most generous," she said at last. "Aunt Eliza has always promised me the Dower Cottage, but to own a farm—" to own a miserable old farm simply because you feel stupidly sentimental about my mother who was probably a whore anyway—her face was an innocent mask of gratitude over the thoughts churning in her head.

"You will not be portionless when you decide to take a husband," he assured her.

"No, indeed. I shall have to beware lest anyone weds me for the sake of my farm," she smiled. "And what of Paget Place? You did mention it."

"The rent it brings in is very little compared with the cost of its upkeep," he said. "I have been hoping for some time to be rid of it eventually, and Miss Browning will not be sorry to move into the town. The manor house is lonely and she is nervous."

"Miss Browning?"

"I have left Paget Place to her," he explained. "Oh, it will not be hers until I am gone, but she may like to spend some part of her time there now."

"How kind you are!" Willow said. "I wonder if anybody in the world is as kind as you!" Fury, black and cold, seethed in her veins. That the wretched governess had been allowed to live in the manor house originally meant for her mother was bad enough, but that she should be given the property in Maidstone was intolerable.

"I have a great admiration for Miss Browning," James said. "She has shown great courage in her adversity."

"Yes, indeed," Willow said fervently.

"And I must ride on. You said Mair has gone home?"

"Yes, she's gone back to *Kingsmead.*"

"And you must stop wandering about in the churchyard," he said teasingly, "else you will grow morbid and pine away your prettiness."

"But you must take care not to die," she warned him. "I couldn't bear it if anything happened to you, Uncle James! There would only be Aunt Eliza then, and she is old."

"Even if anything did happen to me, and it won't, Nathan would always regard you as his dear cousin," he assured her.

"And I would have Wittle Farm, where my own mother was born." And Miss Browning would have Paget Place, she thought, blowing him a kiss as she continued along the path. She takes everything that might have been mine, and yet she is not even a member of the family. It was little wonder that Lady Mair resented the governess and her child, little wonder that she spent long hours in the doctor's company, and that her mouth was envious.

Willow paused, her eyes still fixed on the leaf-strewn ground, as a new idea took shape in her mind. The governess was a threat, not only to her own expectations but to Lady Mair. If she could only find some way to make Lady Mair grateful to her, then the words of the curse would surely be fitting reward.

"And I will claim them," the girl muttered. "I will drive the governess away, and Lady Mair will thank me for it. Uncle James will probably leave Paget Place to me as well as Wittle Farm. I'll have those and the cottage to set up against *Kingsmead* and the manor, and I'll have the words." The words that were the dark heritage of her blood meant more to her than house or cottage or farm. When she finally learned them she would be able to hold up her head as high as any Falcon, and with fully as much pride.

Her lips curved into a pleased smile and she hastened toward the cottage, humming under her breath.

James made his way home more slowly. It was becoming an increasing burden to return to the silence and loneliness of *Kingsmead*. Mair left the room as soon as he entered it, or sat at the table crumbling bread between her fingers and staring resentfully from under her lashes. Yet, apparently, she had the time to spend hours with the doctor. He frowned, recalling Willow's embarrassed manner when she had told him. Perhaps Mair was ill and had not told him. It seemed unlikely, for she had always, even during her confinements, enjoyed excellent health.

Almost with relief he switched his thoughts back to the others for whom he considered himself responsible. Nathan was at school where he would learn to mix with other boys, to forget the unhappiness of the summer past. Aunt Eliza was snug in the cottage with supplies laid in for the winter. He wished he could persuade her to come to *Kingsmead*, but she valued her independence and Mair could scarcely bring herself to be civil to the old lady.

Slowing his horse to a walk, for he had entered the main drive, he thought of Felice Browning and her child. She was a sweet, grateful creature, happy with the small kindnesses he showed her, and she kept the manor house beautifully. He was always sure that when he visited her there would be a blazing fire, fresh-baked biscuits, a hot toddy at his elbow. It was a thousand pities that she was unlikely ever to marry, but she shrank from men now, as if something more than her flesh had been violated. At least he had ensured that when he died she would have a home of her own.

He had reached the arch of the courtyard and paused, as he always did, to touch the leaves of the luck tree. It sprayed its purple-veined, rust-colored leaves against the mellow stone. He had never seen another tree like it, and the thought that it was unique to Falcon land pleased him. Mair had never liked the tree. Had it been her decision, it would have been cut down long since.

Mair, from the upper window of the room that had been Joan's, watched her husband ride into the courtyard. His shoulders were slightly bowed, and the sprinkling of grey at his temples was more pronounced. He had put on a little weight recently, and the lines in his face were deeper. Staring down at him, hating him, she was shaken by a desire for him so intense it was like a physical pain. She clasped her hands together tightly and bit down upon her knuckles.

Since Joan's death she had slept in this room, carefully locking the door of the outer chamber, but no hand had rattled the knob or fumbled for the key. "If he comes to me now," she vowed, "I will forgive him and be a wife again. I'll not visit Guto Evans anymore." She closed her eyes, sucking the thin trickle of blood from her bitten knuckles, holding her breath lest she miss the sound of footsteps on the stairs.

James entered the great hall wearily, shrugging off his caped coat. The staircase loomed ahead of him, its stone stretching up to the gallery above. The portraits of his ancestors hung in formation along the upper wall. He had grown up with the portraits and felt for each one a warm, personal affection. To him they were a tangled reminder of the past that lay all about him and had shaped the fortunes of his family.

There were not many left now, he thought with deep sadness. Of the six children sired by his grandfather, only two had borne fruit. Now, apart from Mair and himself, there were only Nathan, Aunt Eliza, and poor little Willow. He and Mair ought to have another child, to ensure the continuation of the line.

Even as he thought that he turned aside and went heavy-footed into the solar. This room, with the parlor, was part of the original Tudor building, though it had been panelled early in the seventeenth century. James liked the solar and insisted on calling it by its old name, though Mair declared it was unfashionable.

That afternoon the room seemed cold, the fire burning low, the window misted with frost. For the first time he felt himself to be an alien in his own home, as if he had, by his own well-meaning generosity, separated himself from his own traditions. This thought, springing into his mind, startled him, for he was not a subtle man.

Suddenly he could no longer endure to stay in the little room. If he rode over to the manor he could enjoy a few hours of cheerful conversation, and no doubt Miss Browning would offer him supper, and Caro would run to meet him, clasping him about the neck as Joan had once done. The image of his daughter was so vivid in his mind that he strode out into the great hall again, taking up his coat from the chair across which he had flung it, calling over his shoulder to the maidservant who hurried from the kitchen.

"Tell your mistress I shall not be here for supper. There is no need for her to wait up, as I may be late."

Mair, opening her eyes as he left the house and called to John for his horse, burned with a fierce and lonely resentment. "He is going to her," she said aloud, as if the pain became more real when she spoke it. "He is going to Felice Browning, as he always does."

She longed to run after him, to call him back and beg him to ask her for forgiveness. Her hands were already reaching toward him, her lips opening to call his name. Her reflection, seen dimly in the long mirror, was anguished, chestnut hair escaping in long strands about her flushed and desperate face. Her breasts hurt and nausea cramped her stomach. "Even if he came," she said, with pathetic jauntiness, "it would do him no good, for this is the wrong time of the month."

And then she was very still and very cold, as if she had been plunged into ice. In the three months since Joan's funeral, in the three months since Guto Evans had first taken her in his arms, she had not suffered monthly courses.

She went on staring at her reflection, and inside her head a voice moaned silently, With child! With child!

Chapter 11

"You are fast becoming as good a cook as Aunt Eliza," James told Willow, leaning back in his chair and savoring the last morsel of gooseberry tart.

"I like cooking when you're coming to supper," Willow said, smiling. She sat at the other side of the table, her chin propped on her hands, her hair tied in two demure bunches. Beyond the window rain fell steadily, obscuring the clearing, but within the room was warm and bright.

"Aunt Eliza will be soaked when she gets back," she observed, "unless she stays over at the manor."

"Caro isn't very sick, is she?" James asked anxiously.

"A feverish cold, Miss Browning said, but Aunt Eliza took some physic for her. Oh Lord! I forgot."

"Forgot what?"

"Miss Browning's key. She dropped it in the woods a few days ago, and I meant to ask Aunt Eliza to give it back to her."

"Why didn't you give it back to her yourself when you saw her drop it?" he enquired.

"I didn't realize she'd dropped anything at first,"

Willow explained. "She was among the trees as I came alone the bridle path. I was going to call out to her, but she suddenly hurried away. I was going after her when I trod on the key. It was under a little pile of leaves, and by the time I'd picked it up she was gone."

"I can take it if you like," he offered. "I'll be going up to the manor later this evening."

"I hoped you'd stay and keep me company," she pouted prettily.

"If Caro is sick I ought to go up there. Do you have the key?"

"I put it somewhere. Yes, in the dresser drawer!" She rose and went to the dresser, returning with the heavy iron key. "I wonder where it belongs," she said, laying it down on the table. "I mean, it can't open anywhere very important, else she'd have missed it."

"It looks like the key to the old apple store," James said, picking it up.

"At *Kingsmead?*"

"No, at the manor. It's no more than a pit, really, at the back of the house. We used to store apples there, but the soil is too soft and wet, and there was some seepage. The store hasn't been used for years."

"Then why would Miss Browning have the key?"

"I can't imagine." He frowned at it for a moment and then slipped it into his pocket. Something was teasing at the back of his mind, but he could not bring the thought into conscious focus. Without knowing why he asked, "Have you seen any strangers about?"

"In Marie Regina? There are scarcely any visitors here at any time, unless you mean that old gypsy."

"What old gypsy?"

"Last winter—perhaps I ought not to have said anything!" Willow put her hand up to her mouth pulling at her lower lip.

"Said anything about what?"

"She told me not to say."

"Who told you?"

"The old gypsy," Willow said hesitantly. "She was in the churchyard. She asked me if I knew where the governess lived, and she told me not to say anything."

"When was this?" he asked.

"Last January or February. I can't recall exactly when. It went out of my head."

"This woman. Did she say who she was?"

"I don't think so." Willow frowned and shook her head. "No, I'm sure she didn't. She just asked me where the governess lived, and she told me not to say anything to anybody. What has all this to do with the key?"

"Nothing at all, I daresay." He frowned again, thinking of Caro. Of Caro who was afraid of bogeys and had spoken of a lady falling through the ground.

"Did this gypsy go up to the manor?" he asked.

"I suppose so. I didn't see her again. Why?"

"No reason." He reached out and tweaked one of the pale bunches of hair.

"Will Nathan be home for Christmas?" she asked. "I would like to write to him, but I was afraid Lady Mair would object."

"I wish you would call her Aunt Mair," he said faintly irritable.

"She wouldn't like it," Willow said.

"I suppose not." His face was dark for a moment. "But you may certainly write to Nathan. You are cousins, after all."

"Would you like some more gooseberry tart?" she asked brightly.

"Thank you, no. I ought to go."

"To the manor? Won't Lady Mair be anxious if you're late?"

"Lady Mair," he said, with sudden bitterness, "never notices if I am late or not."

She helped him solicitously with his greatcoat and held open the door as he ducked beneath the lintel into the rain. When he had ridden away she closed the door softly and went back to the table.

So far it had been easier than she could have hoped. What happened next depended upon the extent of her uncle's curiosity. Leaning across the table she cut herself a large slice of the gooseberry tart and began to eat it with relish.

James hunched his shoulders against the rain as he rode between the dripping trees up to the bridge. The key lay heavy in his pocket, teasing at his mind. The old apple store. Caro's nightmare. A gypsy asking questions.

When he saw the outlines of the manor house glimmering through the darkness he dismounted and led the horse across the grass to the back of the building. It was foolish and irrational, but it would do no harm to look in the apple store.

A lantern glowed on its hook by the back door. He stepped over and lifted it down, holding it low, and stepped back across the turf to where the sloping door fitted in the ascending ground. He knelt, took the key from his pocket and turned it in the lock. The door lifted creakingly on its hinges and then, lantern swaying over the aperture, he looked down into the water-logged cellar. Yellow bone, empty eye sockets, threads of coarse black hair nestled in the muddy residue of the November rain. In the rotted ears two golden hoops glinted.

He closed the door slowly and quietly, locked it

again, and bent over, retching. His throat was raw and his eyes stung and the reek of corruption was in his nostrils.

He felt stiff and cramped when he rose and his trousers clung wetly to his legs. He hung the lantern back on its hook and walked beneath the trees, shivering a little with cold and shock.

There could only have been one reason for the gypsy woman to seek the governess. The man who had attacked Felice Browning had been a Romany man, and Caro, for all her delicacy of feature, was half-gypsy. The woman had been looking for the child. Somehow or other she had ended here in the old apple store, but what had happened between her arrival at the manor and this disintegration was no more than dark conjecture.

He pictured Felice Browning with her tear-drenched blue eyes and her black curls and her little, helpless, fluttering gestures. It was beyond belief that she could ever have used violence against another human being. The door must have been left open and the woman had misjudged her footing and fallen. But the door had been locked, and Willow had seen Miss Browning drop the key. His mind dealt with the situation slowly and painfully. The gypsy had fallen down into the store and Miss Browning had found her and been so afraid that she had locked it up and tried to throw away the key. But Caro had seen two figures on one horse. He thought of Willow who, despite her smallness, was strong and sinewy. And Willow had always spoken gently of Miss Browning and the child, perhaps because in Caro she had seen something of her own fatherless situation.

In his mind the scene rearranged itself. The gypsy asked Willow where the governess lived, and Willow rode double with the gypsy to the manor house. She had meant only to frighten the woman, or perhaps the horse had reared, and the woman had fallen into the open store. Willow had been terrified, poor maid, and slammed shut the door and galloped back to the cottage. Felice Browning must have found the body and locked the door again and tried to lose the key. Perhaps she was afraid of being blamed for the death, and Willow, knowing that, had tried obliquely to make confession to the man she trusted more than any man. Poor Willow! Poor little Willow!

If there was a flaw in his reasoning his mind paved it over with sympathy for the two young women, with distaste for the thing lying in the water. It would have to be covered up completely, the space filled in with wet, soft earth.

He waited, motionless, hearing after a long time voices from the front of the house, carried by the wind in fragments of conversation. "—be perfectly well in a day or two, if you keep her warm." "—very kind indeed. You're sure that you won't—" "—better for me to start off while there's a lull in the rain. Willow might fret if I didn't get back. Now go inside again, my dear. No sense in your catching cold, too."

Dear Aunt Eliza! He could see her clambering up to the saddle, her turban hat tipping over her blue eyes, her hands firm on the reins. She was all that was left now of his childhood.

Hoofbeats echoed back from the drive and a door slammed. James stayed where he was, waiting. The shutters at the back of the house were closed, and he estimated that within an hour Miss Browning would probably be asleep. Then he would get a spade from the barn and fill up the space with earth and lock the door again. It would be very late when he had finished. For the first time he was glad that Mair had moved into another room.

Mair lay quiet in her lover's arms, listening to the splash of rain upon the eaves. Guto's slim, hard, dark body was as familiar to her now as her own, but there were times, even when he was locked within her, when she wished passionately that upon opening her eyes she would look up into her husband's broad, fair face and sun-licked hair.

"You're putting on weight," Guto said lazily.

"I'm with child," she said, and marvelled that the words brooded over for so long should come out so clearly and simply.

"With child?" He repeated the words very slowly.

"You're a doctor. Didn't you guess?"

"With child," he said again. "You're certain?"

"Of course I'm certain! Haven't I borne two already?" she demanded.

"Is it mine?" he asked.

For a moment she thought she had not heard aright. Then color rushed into her face and she raised herself on one elbow, staring down at him in hurt dismay.

"You must know it's yours," she said. "I told you that James and I haven't lived together since Joan died. Dear God! Of course the child is yours!"

"You'll have to get rid of it," he told her.

"Do you think I've not tried that?" she asked bitterly. "But it's not as easy as folks say."

"When is it due?" He also had half-risen, drawing the covers about his shoulders.

"In April." She swung her legs over the side of the bed and sat shivering.

"Then it's mine. My child."

"Cannot you—cannot you do something? You're a doctor," she pleaded.

"I swore to save life, not to end it," he said sharply.

"Then we will have to go away together," she said, twisting her hands together. "James is a good man, a tolerant man, but even he could not be expected to claim a babe he has not fathered."

"And you could not hope to deceive him."

"It would be impossible," she said miserably, "and even if it were possible, I wouldn't do such a thing."

"Then you still love him," he said.

"No, it's you I love!" she said violently. "It's you, Guto. I love you."

He was silent, hunched in the bed, gazing at her, and she bent down, catching his black head in her hands, kissing him passionately, though, at that moment, she could not have told whether she was trying to force warmth out of her own heart or his.

"I love you, too," he said at last.

"Then we'll go away together." She was dressing feverishly as she spoke, her moist hands slipping on laces and ribbons.

"Go where?"

"I have land in Wales, in the north," she said eagerly. "The little farm where I was born and grew up. They need a doctor there. The local one will be old by now."

"I would lose my licence to practise medicine," he said bleakly.

"Then you can work the farm," she said. "The soil isn't good, too marshy, but we can clear the ground and buy fresh stock. My parents went to Saron when they ran away to wed."

"We wouldn't be wed."

"Nobody would know, and James might divorce me. He would have grounds enough to lay before Parliament."

He was so angry that he was afraid to move lest
he struck her. She was a cow, a stupid cow! She had
no idea in the world what it meant to be born part
gypsy, to fight one's way through medical school, to
learn how to dress correctly and speak like a gentleman. She really expected him to run away from the
image of himself that he had created, to drop his
ambitions as casually as he might drop a handker-
chief, to risk social disgrace and professional oblivion,
even possible arrest for abduction.

"We would be happy," she said. "I was reared on a
farm. I know how to work, believe me."

She had, he thought, large feet and hands, an abun-
dance of fecund vitality, a coarseness of complexion
that belied her ladylike manners. She was generous
and passionate and had excited him at first, but recently her lack of discretion had begun to alarm him,
her possessiveness to suffocate him.

"We will be happy," she said, pushing back her
mane of hair. "We will be happy, Guto, if we're together. James won't follow us, won't try to find us. He
has too much pride."

"We will talk of this later," he evaded.

"And make plans, yes." She flung her mantle around
her shoulders and stared at him hungrily. "I have
no money of my own, but I have some jewels that my
husband gave me when we were wed. And I can live
simply, very simply. You will see."

"Where did you leave your horse?" he interrupted.

"In the churchyard, as usual."

"You will get soaked in this rain," he cautioned her.
"Milord may notice."

"Milord never notices if I am at home or absent,"
she said bitterly. "He went down to the Dower Cottage for supper tonight. It will be late when he rides

back to *Kingsmead*, and then he will sleep until dawn and rise early to see to the duties of the estate. One would imagine that he had not the means to employ laborers!"

"What of Náthan?" he asked. "What of your son?"

She caught her breath as if she were in pain, and then said coldly, "Nathan is not a child. He is away at school now with boys of his own age. He will forget me."

"And your husband?"

"He has forgotten me already," she said, and her lip quivered.

When she had gone Guto lay down again, curling into the warm space left by her body. He felt sick and tired, weary of all women, angry with himself for having been fool enough to take advantage of her loneliness in order to seduce her. As a physician he had known quite well that there was always the chance of a baby, but he had credited her with enough sense to tempt her husband back into her bed so that any child would be acknowledged as his.

He flexed his thin, muscular hands and looked at them critically. They were good hands, doctor's hands, hands trained for healing. He had used them instead to caress a woman, and that caress, if he did not act promptly, would lead to disaster. After a little while he rose and began to dress.

Mair, hooded and cloaked, trod softly past the sleeping parsonage to the drenched stones and weeping yews of the graveyard. The rain had eased and a thin silver moon struggled through lowering clouds. At the Falcon tomb the angel stood night-guard, diamonds of rain glinting from his sword. She paused, remembering her horror when they had opened the triple-locked door and laid Joan within. Merry, smiling

Joan, who had never caused anybody a moment's pain, and now lay locked in stone, an angel preventing escape, amid the bones of her ancestors.

And I will never join you, Mair thought in swift and painful anguish. I have forfeited the right to lie with my people, just as I have forfeited the right to live at *Kingsmead*. At that moment she wanted James so desperately that it was like a fierce hunger tearing at her bowels. She wanted her head on his shoulder and his arms about her, as it had been in the days before the governess came, but when she leaned her head sideways it touched the cold, wet stone of the angel, in whom there was no comfort.

She roused herself and mounted her horse and rode slowly across the field. The moon was brightening the dark landscape now, and the wind was gentle. Another rider was coming along the main road, across the bridge. She reined in her own mount under the shadow of an oak and stayed, motionless, watching James ride past, coming from the direction of the manor house. A brief flash of moonlight revealed muddied boots and rain-sodden greatcoat, and then he was past her, never noticing, never turning his head. And the wind was harsh again, and even the stone angel would have been better comfort than none at all.

It is done, James thought, his shoulders aching with tiredness. The apple store was half-filled in with wet, black, concealing earth, the door relocked and the key safe in his pocket. Somehow he would find words with which to reassure both Willow and Miss Browning that their separate actions would remain hidden from knowledge. Meanwhile, he was tired and wet and cold, mindful of the fact that he would have to enter the house quietly lest he disturb Mair. She had looked ill recently, dark circles under her eyes, her waist thickening. He wanted to put his arms round her and tell her he loved her, but it was quite useless. She would only push him away.

At the manor house Felice woke briefly, raising herself on one elbow and listening. Something had woken her, but Caro slept peacefully, her feverish coughing stilled. Yet something had woken her. She had been dreaming of her father, of him sitting at a table and slapping down cards on it. Red and black, black and red, and every one had the face of Lord Falcon. The sound of the cards was like wet earth being dropped from a spade, and then a horse had ridden into her dream, and she was awake. After a moment or two she lay down and closed her eyes, willing herself to dream once more.

Eliza slept without dreams, her mind a tranquil well in which neither conscience nor desire had dominion. Her flowered nightcap had slipped to one side and curly grey hair, silvered by the moon to a pale shadow of its original bright gold, feathered her serene brow. If any stray thought invaded her slumber, it was a vague feeling of contentment. Mair was pregnant again, if Eliza's instincts had not failed her, and that meant there had been a private reconciliation between her and James. There would be another child to help to sweeten the grief that Joan's death had brought. A smile twitched the corners of Eliza's mouth. Momentarily she looked like a girl again.

Willow, who slept as fitfully as a cat, was awake, listening to each small, separate sound. Rain dripping from the eaves swept down the windowpane. The river ran high, gurgling over boulders. The bucket that hung at the side of the cottage creaked dolefully as it swung in the wind.

When Uncle James opens the apple store he will find the gypsy and imagine that Miss Browning put her there and threw away the key, Willow thought. Even if he doesn't lay information against her to the authorities, he will surely not allow her to go on living at the manor house. And he will change his will again and not leave Paget Place to her.

He might even leave it to Willow herself. Fired by this idea the girl sprang up and went to the window, rubbing the misted panes with the edge of her sleeve. The clearing beyond was mute under the swirling sky, though its fringe of trees and bushes quivered and shook as if each separate twig and leaf danced to a secret, primeval measure of its own.

She unhasped the casement and leaned out, the wind cold on her small, pale face, a shower of errant raindrops cascading about her.

"Oh, Lilith, Queen of the dark side of the moon! I crave to be loved and to possess. You, who dwelt in Eden before Eve was formed, lend me your subtle strength. Make me one day mistress over *Kingsmead* itself, and give me the curse words so that I may use them against those who will not love me." Fragile words, whispered into the moonshot dark, and the black stone was burning ice in her hands.

A figure stood beneath the window, listening. Willow became aware of it by degrees, as if it built itself up out of the wind and the rain and her own scarlet desires.

The girl was tiny, with black hair that fell in tangles to the hem of her gown, and her eyes were yellow, as wide and yellow as a cat's eyes.

"Margred? Are you the witch Margred? She who first bore the devil's kiss upon her thigh and cursed this family down the centuries?" Willow spoke urgently, her heart thumping, her mouth dry. "Give me the words," she begged. "In the name of Lilith, teach me the words."

The figure raised thin arms and opened its mouth, but no sound came forth save a faint gasping, as if the long journey from the grave had exhausted all speech.

The moon was gone behind a cloud and the black stone was heavy and the figure had splintered again into rain and wind and the dark places of the soul.

Chapter 12

"But it's not possible," Mair said blankly. Her hair strayed wispily from beneath her hat, and her skirts were covered with dust.

"Dr. Evans rode out early this morning, Lady Falcon," Mr. Penn said. "He left the keys of the house in my charge, and the next quarters' rent, which he said falls due at the end of next month."

"So he's coming back?" Her heart lifted in hope.

"I don't think so, milady. He said he'd been called away to a sick relative, that he'd often think of us kindly when he was settled in his new practice." Mr. Penn was neither an observant nor an inquisitive man, but it was dawning on him slowly that Lady Falcon was looking positively ill.

"Is anything wrong, milady?" he enquired anxiously. "Did you need the physician?"

"No, no. I wished to renew the prescription he gave me for my nerves, that's all," she said hastily.

"I'm sorry to hear you are not well." He peered at her in solicitude. It seemed to him that she had faced the loss of her daughter with truly Christian fortitude,

165

but shock was sometimes delayed, and the poor lady did look ill.

"It is merely the time of the year," she said vaguely. "So, the doctor has left us?"

"But surely you knew something of it?" he said in surprise.

"Yes, of course. Certainly I knew. I must have misunderstood the day he mentioned as his departure day."

"And he forgot to give you the rent and the keys. Fortunately, I can hand everything over to you intact, as I do now, milady." With spectacles glinting on nose, he beamed at her. "We must hope his aunt is soon recovered."

"Yes, indeed."

"And he left no renewal of your prescription! If you have a little left in the bottle. I'm certain the druggist at Maidstone would remember the formula and have it made up again for you."

"Yes. I'll have John see to it," she said automatically.

"We must send good wishes after our medical friend, eh, Lady Falcon? Not that I had cause for his services, myself. The Lord be praised, but I have an excellent constitution. Indeed, there's no denying his practice here was very small. People are slow to accept new methods, new ways. The pace of life must have seemed a mite old-fashioned to him, perhaps. Country ways, country manners, eh, milady?" Smiling, taking off his spectacles to polish them, rocking to and fro on his broad, flat feet. Her heart was breaking, and he could not hear it crack.

"If you will excuse me, Mr. Penn, I ought to be going." She climbed back into the pony trap, feeling the heaviness of unborn life drag at her belly. Under her eyes the shadows were black.

"Is Master Nathan well? Not falling behind in his Latin and Greek, I hope?"

"After your excellent grounding that would be very difficult," she said, arranging her mouth into a smile.

"Please remember me to him when you write. He will be at home for the festive season, I take it?"

"The festive—Oh, Christmas. Yes, Nathan will be home for Christmas." She nodded, still smiling, and slapped the reins across the pony's broad back. Inside, she was disintegrating, dying.

"At least the weather has cleared up nicely," Mr. Penn called after her.

The rain had ceased hours before, blown away by the cold wind, the slivers of ice decorated the entwined foliage of hedge and woodland. The sky was a clear, frost-bitten blue, innocent of cloud.

On the main road she jerked the pony to a halt and bowed her head, allowing misery to overwhelm her.

"Mair? Are you not well? Is something wrong?" James had clattered over the bridge behind her and drawn rein at the side of the trap.

"I am tired," she said flatly, raising her head.

"Tired? Why, what do you do to make you so tired?" he asked in surprise.

"I wait up for you to come riding home in the middle of the night," she said angrily.

"I made no noise, and there was no light in your room," he said unwisely.

"The very soul of a considerate husband!" Mair mocked. "And where had you been till that hour? Not down at the Dower Cottage, I'll swear. Aunt Eliza and Willow Clegg don't keep such late hours."

"I was riding."

"In the pouring rain? You went to the manor house, didn't you? You went to see the governess."

"I assure you, my dear, that I never spoke to Miss Browning last evening."

"That governess and her gypsy bastard! You went to see her, to spend half the night with her!"

"You are mistaken," he said mildly, but his fair complexion had reddened and his eyes avoided hers.

"I am not mistaken!" She lashed her mood into fury. Better anger than pain. "You were with that woman, as you were with her on the night that Joan died. She's your mistress, isn't she? Felice Browning is your mistress."

"That's ridiculous! She's under my protection, that is all."

"A pretty way to put it, but then Felice Browning is a pretty creature, isn't she? Pretty and sly and clinging with her big, blue eyes and her Frenchified manners! And you engaged her, you did engage her in the beginning. And you cannot keep away from her, can you?"

"At least when I visit Miss Browning she greets me pleasantly and is not forever scowling at me and turning her back," he said, stung by Mair's goading into a rare display of temper.

"You're in love with her," she accused. "I know it. I know it."

"That's ridiculous," he said again. "I have merely been kind to the poor young woman."

"By letting her live in the manor house, by visiting her at all hours of the night and day, by treating her bastard as if it were your own? I suppose you will be leaving the house to her when you die, in case I get the notion of turning her out-of-doors!"

"I am leaving her Paget Place," he said, too angry

to be discreet. "She will have Paget Place when I am gone."

"The townhouse? Have you lost your senses completely?" she cried. "It is part of the Falcon estate."

"But not part of the original entail. I may leave it where I choose."

"And what, pray, am I to be given?" she demanded. "Wittle Farm, I suppose."

"The farm is for Willow. Her mother was born there."

"Huldah Clegg, who stole your affections when you were a boy and betrayed you with your own brother! Willow and Miss Browning may count themselves fortunate that you are so sentimental, my dear husband."

"You are being foolish," he said, breathing heavily. "You will have the manor house after Nathan is wed."

"The manor house, which you prepared for Huldah Clegg, and where your mistress now lives? I'd burn it down about her ears before I'd humble my pride into such shame!"

"The whole village will hear you. Keep your voice down," he begged.

In reply, she whipped up the pony savagely and sent the trap careering up the road, bumping from side to side. James wiped the back of his hand across his forehead and shivered, his anger draining into dismay. He had been a complete fool to tell Mair his intentions. She had always been proud of the estate, of the number of houses he owned, the extent of his land. And she was jealous of anybody whom he liked or to whom he showed kindness.

After a moment he clicked his tongue and rode on slowly, following the swaying pony trap.

Below the level of the road, pressed up against the trunk of a tree, Willow stood, arms wrapped about herself, pale hair falling over the collar of her long cape. She had heard every word exchanged between her uncle and his wife, every word had been as clear as a bell, clashing together in her mind.

Whether he had opened the apple store or not, it was plain that he still intended to leave Paget Place to the governess and her brat. And Lady Mair was to have the manor house. That hadn't pleased her, Willow thought, her lips curving into a bitter little grin. She had declared that she would burn the place about Miss Browning's ears rather than live there after James was dead. Burn it down, burn it down, burn it down. The words sang inside her head. Burn, burn, *burn*.

If the house were to burn, then Lady Mair would be blamed for it. And Felice Browning and the child might both die. And there would only be Willow Clegg to have Paget Place, as well as Wittle Farm and the Dower Cottage.

She walked slowly between the trees, bending her head under the water-laden, ice-frilled branches. She was thinking carefully, her sharp brain selecting and discarding various schemes. She had an idea that in the end the simplest plan would be the most effective.

Mair, clambering down from the trap, ran clumsily through the main door of *Kingsmead*. If James caught up with her now she might be tempted to shout out more and more abuse, and not all of it would be meant, because part of her still clung to the habit of loving him.

Safe in her own room, the door locked against pursuit, she flung herself on the bed, weeping noisily, tearing at the coverlet with unhappy hands. She had never thought for a moment that Guto would ever leave her. In some part of her mind was the conviction that all men were as honorable as James. Honorable, and generous! Well, she had need of his generosity now. She shrank from the prospect of telling him, shrank from the hurt bewilderment on his face. Even though she had no doubt that he would forgive her and accept the coming child as his own, nothing would ever be the same between them again.

A long time afterward she heard James ride out again. He had not followed her after all, not tried to enter her room. She sat up, rubbing her swollen eyelids, pushing back her tangled hair. The long mirror reflected a plain, middle-aged woman whom no man could love.

As a girl on the tiny farm where her parents had lived, she had often walked and ridden for hours in the silent countryside. The need to be away from the house and its carefully tended grounds overwhelmed her again. It would be sweet to return for a few hours to the uncomplicated rhythms of her youth. She pulled off her dress, averting her eyes from her thickening waist, and rummaged in the closet for a riding habit.

It was dark soon after four o'clock that afternoon, the frost thickening on the roads, the waters of the river white-foamed, the houses seeming to huddle together as if for warmth. James, arriving back at *Kingsmead* after a lengthy afternoon argument with a recalcitrant wheelwright who was vainly trying to raise his prices, was informed by Betsy that Lady Mair had ridden out earlier.

"On Diamond, milord. And you know how skittish Diamond can be, with frost on the road and the darkness coming up!"

"Did she say where she was going?"

"No, milord. She only said not to wait supper. Will

you be having your supper now, sir? There's a mutton pie," she tempted him.

"Later. I'm not hungry." He gave her his brief, sweet smile.

"As if he knew," Betsy said later to Cook, "that something terrible was going to happen."

"I always did say the Falcons had a strange, seeing way about them," Cook said.

But that was later, much later. For the present Betsy took James's greatcoat, bobbed a curtsey, and hurried back to the kitchen where a bright fire blazed. James went through to the long, elegant drawing-room where he sat staring into the flames of a feeble blaze, thinking of his wife.

Aunt Eliza was enjoying a mug of special punch. Skirt tucked up over her knees to display still-shapely legs, mobcap pulled down over her ears, she sipped appreciatively at the steaming liquid. Willow brewed punch to perfection. She did most things neatly and gracefully, and recently she had begun to grow out of her habit of wandering about with no particular purpose.

Watching the girl, as she sat by the window gazing out into the clearing, Eliza thought, She needs more company, more young folk about her. She will have to marry somebody one day. It's selfish of me to keep her close with me.

She yawned suddenly, aware of a slight blurring of vision. Surely she did not require spectacles already! The Falcons had eyes as sharp as their feathered namesakes, and she was not yet sixty-seven years old.

"Are you tired, Aunt dear?" The girl's voice cooed at her through the haze of hot punch and warm firelight. Willow was playing with something black and shiny, tossing it from hand to hand. Eliza had glimpsed it before, and wondered vaguely what it was.

"Think I'll have a little nap," she decided aloud.

"Finish your punch. I brewed it specially for you."

"The punch. Oh, yes." She drained the mug, conscious of a faint bitterness tingling on the end of her tongue. "Are you going out?"

"Tonight? No, only to the stable to check on the feed. I thought it was a little low."

Willow took the mug and rinsed it carefully. Eliza leaned back against the cushions of the rocking chair, her eyes closed, her breathing regular, her hands loose in her lap.

Willow took down her cape and opened the door cautiously. Aunt Eliza would sleep now for an hour or two at least, and Willow's task would take no more than an hour if she took the shortest way over the bridge and across the fields to the manor house.

It was a clear, starlit evening, an evening for lovers muffled in furs, clinging hand to hand, mouth to mouth. But some of us are not framed for love, Willow thought as she ran zigzag between the moon-gleamed trees. Some of us were framed for the dark.

The lower windows of the manor house were in darkness, but a light flared from the upper storey. Felice Browning would be putting Caro to bed, reading her a story, singing her a lullaby. The little deaf servant girl was already curled up on her narrow bed, ready for her regular dawn rising with hearths to be cleared, water boiled, stove leaded.

The back door was locked, but the pantry window was child's play to unlatch. Willow slipped through the narrow aperture without difficulty and stood on the stone floor. Beyond the half-open door the kitchen was dim, with no sound in it save the snoring of the maid.

She moved, swift and feather-footed, into the main hall. There was always the danger that Felice Browning might come down the stairs, but the risk was small. She went into the parlor where the fire burned brightly and candles were ready for the lighting. The sewing box stood open on a table at the side of a wing-backed chair. In a box by the hearth small logs were piled high.

Comfort, ease, elegance—intended for a bailiff's daughter, enjoyed now by the governess, meant for the haughty Welsh wife. Willow's lip lifted in contempt as she took a length of log and thrust it deep into the glowing heart of the fire.

When it was kindled, when red and gold tongues of flame licked out from the smooth bark, she rose without haste and moved about the room, touching the burning end to curtains, covers, sewing box, rug, tapestry frame. Out in the hall again, to slide the burning brand up and down the panelled walls, along the carpet that covered the wooden stair treads. The manor house had been well maintained in the centuries since its construction. The wood was dry, the hangings of fine silk, the furniture so lightly carved and varnished that it blazed up without falter.

She allowed herself one brief moment in which to admire her work. Then she flung the flaming log into the sheet of fire that rose up at the foot of the stairs and went swiftly back into the kitchen again. As she eased herself through the window the maidservant stirred in her sleep and coughed.

Willow sped back through the grounds without looking back at the manor house. Only when she was safely across the bridge, plunging down the bridle path, did she glance up and smile to see the spangled sky glowing red, as if some shepherd heralded a joyful night.

Eliza still slept, her skirt tucked over her knees, her mobcap tipping ever further over one eye. The fire in the hearth had sunk into red ash and white skeleton-fingers of wood. Willow hung up her cloak, laid fresh wood on the fire, and sat down with her head against the older woman's leg. Curled like a kitten, her sea-colored eyes dreaming into the rekindled fire, she took the black stone out of her pocket and held it, close and loving, between the narrow palms of her small hands.

"If you please, milord, the sky is all lit up, and John says do you think they've lighted the beacon because we've gone to war again?" Betsy's voice disturbed James from a troubled doze. He woke with a start from a dream of Mair weeping as she galloped through a tangled forest, and blinked at the maid in confusion.

"War? What are you talking about?" he demanded, struggling upright.

"The sky is all lit up, sir, and John says—"

"I heard." He went over to the long windows, opened them and stepped out to the lawn.

Away to the right, beyond the trees and the river, the sky glowed as if some premature dawn had banished the night. He stared at it for a moment and then began to run toward the stables, calling for his horse as he went.

Mair, riding slowly back from Maidstone, drew rein as she frowned into the glowing sky. She had been riding aimlessly for hours, her mind heavy with pain, her head aching with its weight of troubling thoughts. In the town she had wandered from shop to shop, gazing through the windows without seeing any of the objects laid out on display. She had decided to enter a coffeehouse for a meal, but the smell of the roasting beans had made her feel sick, and she had turned away, gone back to the stabling yard and remounted Diamond, and ridden back toward Marie Regina with dread in her heart.

People were running up from the village, clutching buckets and pails and brooms. She was abruptly in the midst of them, and then they surged past her like waves, and she was isolated again on her private rock of despair.

The Vicar panted up, his hat askew, his spectacles dangling forgotten on the end of their chain.

"A terrible, terrible thing, milady," he gasped out. "They say the whole house has gone up in flames. It must be an accident. Nobody could be so wicked as to do such a shocking thing deliberately."

"No, indeed," she said calmly, and watched him hurry past.

James would believe that she had started the fire. Had she not cried out something about burning the manor house down about Miss Browning's ears? But she had spoken in temper, not meaning it. But James would remember. No hope now of confessing and begging him to acknowledge her bastard child as his own. Whether he loved the governess or not, if anything had happened to her—she bent her head, her lips moving silently.

"The child is safe. Miss Browning threw her from the upper window into a pile of bracken."

"Cut and bruised, but crying too loudly to be much hurt."

"No hope for the poor governess now. The roof has gone."

"They're bringing out the maid's body."

"She must have run back into the hall to try to warn Miss Browning."

"A terrible, terrible tragedy!"

Words shouted past her into the icy air; faces, shocked and sympathetic, full, in some cases, of a secret glee in the excitement of another's misfortune; feet, hurrying with bad news. The sky darkening again as the fire began to wither into ash and black smoke crowned the midnight horizon.

It was over, then. It was all over. The curse laid upon the Falcons by the woman who had come out of Wales had reached down at last, sweeping away all hope of happiness.

The words of the curse echoed in her mind like pebbles in a hollow cave, sharp and stinging and cruel. She had learned them from her mother while she lay dying, and they were as harsh and clear now as when they had dropped from Apple's pale lips.

"Grow, little vinegar tree! Grow tall and strong and overshadow the house of Falcon. Let them taste the bitterness of your leaves, in season and out of season, by night and by day, in sun and rain, in wind and snow. Let them bleed from your branches and tangle their hearts in your roots—"

Sobbing dryly, she lashed Diamond with her whip and galloped off toward Maidstone again. The London coach left at dawn and from London she could make her way northwest, back to the little farm.

If James ever discovered the truth, or decided to

forgive her, she would have to be in a place where he could find her. As she rode it began to snow, lightly at first, and then more heavily, as if the elements set their own seal on her resolution.

"She went like the wind," somebody would say the next day. "Like the wind, as if the hounds of hell were baying at her back."

"Guilt all over her face."

"Of course, we all know that she disliked Miss Browning. Jealous of a younger woman, that's what it was. Not that she'd any cause, for there's no more honorable gentleman in the whole of Kent than Lord Falcon."

"The child is to be brought up at *Kingsmead,* they say. There's talk of a governess being engaged for her, on account of Miss Eliza being too old to rear a small child."

"Master Nathan won't come home this Yuletide, I'm thinking."

"Poor young man. I wonder what they'll say at the inquest on the governess."

"Accidental death, you'll see. It will all be hushed up, for the sake of the family honor."

So the whispers ran, while the falling snow covered the gaunt skeleton of the manor house. At *Kingsmead* James sat alone in the solar, his eyes red-rimmed with fatigue and tears. In the room where Joan and, more recently, Mair had slept, Caro Browning was tucked in, thumb in her mouth, cuts healing on her small face. Later on James would begin to plan her future, but for the moment he could only sit, shoulders hunched, numb with grief and shock, and think of Mair and the look on her face when she threatened to burn down the manor house.

In the Dower Cottage Aunt Eliza wept for the

little black-haired governess whose life had been cut so cruelly short. And Willow shook her head in pity, pale hair shielding her cheeks, and tossed the black stone from hand to hand.

PART III
1835

Chapter 13

Spring had erupted in a million blossoms that spangled the greening leaves as if a multitude of brides sprang out of the warm earth. The sky was a clear, truthful blue, tinged with the gold of the afternoon sun, unmarred by cloud.

"A fine day for a journey!" the plump man said cheerfully.

The other occupants of the stagecoach nodded, infected by the general air of comradeship that had prevailed since the journey's beginning in London. Not all the bouncing and jolting in the world could alter the fact that it was spring.

"A fine day, indeed," the woman in the corner said, settling her basket more firmly on her lap. "I'm bound for Maidstone to visit my daughter. She's just had her first. A dear little boy. Pretty fellow."

"It's at such times that a girl needs her mother," another of the female passengers said.

"Are you travelling as far as Maidstone, sir?" The plump gentleman, leaning forward to address the young man seated opposite him, unconsciously lowered his voice in deference to the other's aristocratic appearance.

"No, sir. I go only as far as Marie Regina," the young man said politely.

"You are not a native of these parts, sir?"

"I was born here, but these last thirteen years I have travelled widely," the young man said, and averted his face slightly, thus conveying his disinclination to continue the conversation.

A handsome gentleman, the plump individual thought, studying him covertly. The near side of thirty, well-dressed, plenty of breeding. Aloud he said, "You'll be pleased to see your family again, I daresay. Parents still hale and hearty, I trust?"

"My father is alive," the young man said shortly, without turning his head. He must be nearly sixty now. I wonder if he ever thinks of my mother. I wonder if she is still alive. Nearly thirteen years and no word from her. No real explanation as to why she left. His mind went back to that afternoon in the headmaster's study. He could still see quite clearly the panelled walls, the scruffed patch on the carpet in front of the desk where generations of schoolboys had fidgeted. The headmaster had cleared his throat several times in his embarrassment, and glanced up and down from the letter he held in his hand.

"A very sad and mysterious affair, my boy. The manor house on your family estate burned down. A young lady and a maidservant killed. Better, in view of your parent's separation, that you remain at school during the Christmas leave."

The phrases were like hammer blows falling on the head of a bewildered fourteen-year-old. Not even when his father came did the situation become clear.

James looked tired and ill, drained of life in a way that his son had never seen and could not understand.

"Your mother has gone away. We must not condemn her for doing what she wished to do, but it pains me to speak of her. Better if we consider her . . . dead."

He could not believe that it was his father speaking. He could not believe that this man with the tired eyes and the bitter mouth was the indulgent father who had romped with him when he was small, held him on his first pony.

"You are my only son and heir," James was saying. "You are a Falcon, and I begin to think that the old tale of a curse upon us was true. It will ease my mind somewhat if you don't come home for some considerable time. Perhaps in your absence the ill-luck will weaken, lose its hold."

He had wanted to ask many questions, to discover what the burning of the manor house and the deaths of Miss Browning and the servant had to do with his mother's departure, but his father had kissed him hastily and gone away, as if he could bear no more.

Thirteen years ago, and in all that time no more visits, as if James feared that he carried some infection within himself that could harm his son. There had been a handsome allowance that provided books, clothes, horses, amusements. There had been long letters filled with news—the crops were doing well or ill, Aunt Eliza had shocked the neighborhood by donning a divided skirt and a silk hat; Caro was to be sent away to school in the autumn; Willow was being urged to look about for a husband and was steadfastly declaring she wished to die an old maid. Never a word about his mother or where she was or if her husband still thought of her in the long evenings when he sat in the elegant drawing-room at *Kingsmead*.

"A noted philanthropist."

Nathan jumped, conscious that the fat man had been talking to him again. "I beg your pardon, sir?"

"I was just observing that we have passed the gates of Lord Falcon's estate. A noted philanthropist and an ardent supporter of the Reform Bill."

"Wasn't there some scandal connected with the family?" The lady with the straw basket lowered her voice. "I do recall hearing that his wife ran away. Some trouble about a governess, I believe. Oh, years ago, and it was all hushed up."

They were rattling toward the wooden bridge. The village lay in its hollow below the level of the road. To the side of the road, trees spilled pink and white flowerets over the bridle path.

"You asked to be set down here, sir." The stage had drawn up and the coachman's round, red face appeared at the window.

"Good-day to you." Nathan spoke politely as he climbed down into the road, and reached up for his luggage. A small overnight bag held the necessities for his journey. If his welcome were sufficiently hearty he would have the rest of his belongings sent on from his London lodgings. He had already made enquiry at his father's club, to be told that Lord Falcon was out of town.

The stagecoach rolled on across the bridge and began the pull up the brow of the hill. He stood still, looking about him, drawing together the strands of his childhood memories. He had not looked through the open gates of *Kingsmead* as they passed, but he could remember the curving drive with its border of oaks and elms. Beyond the bridge the driveway to the manor house curved, also beyond open gates. He turned his gaze toward the village, seeing from where he stood the roofs of the houses, the tall spire of the church behind which the grey headstones clustered, the ribbon of river below the ruin-crowned hill. He seemed at that moment to stand at the center of all his past life, and everything he had ever known or felt was spread out around him.

"Nathan? Surely it's Nathan!" He turned slowly and watched the slim, small figure glide gracefully up from the bridle path. In thirteen years fashions had changed, slender high-waisted dresses giving way to bunched skirts and puffed sleeves and tiny straw bonnets. But Willow herself had not changed. Her skin was still pale and perfect; her hair, looped about her ears, held in its coils the silver gleam of moonlight; her eyes were no color and all colors.

"Nathan?" she said again and put out her hands toward him.

"Cousin Willow! How did you recognize me?" he exclaimed.

"I've been hoping for years that you would get down from the stage one day," she said, presenting a smooth cheek for his kiss. "And now you are here and I knew you at once. You have not altered so very much, you know." She was gazing at him with shy admiration, studying the lean planes of cheekbone and jaw, the intensely blue eyes under the thatch of nut-brown hair.

"And I would have known you anywhere," he returned.

"I don't change very much," she said with a faint shrug. "But I am an old maid now, you know, like Aunt Eliza."

"How is Aunt Eliza?" he asked eagerly.

"Close on eighty and has more energy than a woman of forty!" Willow laughed, showing her pretty teeth.

"She is over at Maidstone today, having a back tooth drawn, and grumbling mightily about it. She will probably stay over there and ride home in the morning. Have you been to *Kingsmead?*"

He shook his head.

"Come to the Dower Cottage first," she invited. "You can have something to eat and drink and catch up on the village gossip. Later you can go to *Kingsmead.*"

It was too great a temptation. He hesitated only an instant and then nodded, smiling. As they stepped down onto the steep, narrow path she gave him her small, cool, ringless hand.

The cottage had not altered at all. Staring at it as they walked across the clearing, Nathan felt as if time had run backward, and he was a boy again, coming down to see his aunt, knowing that his mother would disapprove.

Willow pushed open the door and he followed her inside. It was not quite the same after all. Everything was smaller than he remembered, subtly diminished by the years. He sat down in the rocking chair and stretched out his legs, watching as she took off her pelisse and began to move about, setting the table, bringing meat and bread from the cupboard. Her gestures were neat and deft, her face unlined.

"Why haven't you married?" he asked abruptly.

"Because nobody ever asked me," she said lightly.

"You ought to have travelled," he said.

"It might have been pleasant," she admitted, "but there was Aunt Eliza, you see. She insists on living here, though Uncle James has asked her again and again to move to the big house. And though she swears that she values her independence, I know she would miss me sadly if I went."

"You have been very dutiful," he said quietly.

"It was not hard. She has always treated me as if I were her own," Willow said. "Uncle James, too. He has always been most generous. Come now. Eat."

She drew a small table up to his elbow and passed over dishes with a solicitous, coaxing air. Imperceptibly Nathan began to relax, began to be able to admit to himself that he had both dreaded and anticipated this return.

Willow poured wine, put the decanter within his reach, and sat down opposite him, her pointed chin resting lightly on her clasped hands. "You have been all over the world," she observed. "It must be strange to come back here."

"Hardly all over the world," he objected, amused. "In Europe, yes."

"Paris, Rome, Vienna," she breathed. "And I have been no further than Maidstone in my life!"

"Travel palls after a while," he said. "The time comes when a man has to return home to take his share of the responsibilities of the estate."

"Your father doesn't know that you're coming?"

"No. I planned to surprise him," Nathan said. "But after all these years—"

"He will welcome you." She rose swiftly and came to his side. "He is so proud of you, cousin. You did so well at school and at Oxford. He never stopped praising you. Your letters are read to us over and over."

"Yet he has always discouraged me from coming home," Nathan said.

"Because he wished you to be free, not to be reminded of past sorrow," she said earnestly. "But it's right that you should come home now. Uncle James is a lonely man."

Nathan frowned into his glass and asked abruptly, "My mother—does he ever speak of my mother?"

"Not once, in all the years since she left."

"And from her?"

"Silence," said Willow. After a moment she continued. "She rode to Maidstone, you know, on the night that the manor was burned. She left her horse at a stable there and took the London coach. The driver said she gave him a diamond ring as payment."

"And Miss Browning was killed."

"She and the poor little deaf servant. It was terrible," Willow said. "The whole house was gutted. A burning log rolled out of the fireplace in the parlor. That was what was said at the inquest."

"My mother disliked Miss Browning," Nathan said. "Even as a boy I was aware of that."

"Jealousy is a dreadful thing," Willow said. Her face was sad and gentle. He had a sudden impulse to touch the thick braids of pale hair coiling like blonde serpents about her ears.

"I can hear somebody coming," she said, and sprang up lightly, gliding to the door.

It was James. Nathan heard his father's voice, deeper and more resonant than in memory, and then Willow went out into the clearing and he heard her sweet, belllike tone and an answering exclamation.

"Nathan! My dear boy, are you really come home?" James was stooping beneath the lintel, his arms outstretched, his face so full of delight that he seemed no different.

"Are you pleased to see me, Father?" Nathan asked uncertainly.

"Pleased? My dear boy, I am absolutely delighted! But you ought to have sent word of your coming.

It's the nearest chance that I was not over at Maidstone with Aunt Eliza. She has gone to the toothdrawer, and I was in a mind to accompany her. But you have grown! Look at him, Willow. He is tremendously grown!" After the initial embrace, James stepped back, his arms falling to his sides again, his expression suddenly bewildered.

"You did not imagine that I would stay fourteen forever, did you?" Nathan asked affectionately.

"But the years have gone by so swiftly," James said, and looked about him as if the errant years were concealed somewhere in the cottage.

He had aged after all, his thick hair receding and almost completely grey, pouches of flesh under his eyes. The ruddy health of his cheeks was purpling into the skin of an elderly man, and there was a faint greyness about his mouth. Old and defeated, Nathan thought in sorrow, and shook his father's hand vigorously all over again.

"Willow is not changed," he said, to cover the emotion of the moment.

"Willow never changes," James said, with a fond glance. "Caro, now, is—"

"Caro?" For a moment Nathan looked blank.

"Caro Browning," Willow said. "You remember, Miss Browning's daughter."

"Yes, of course. But she was just a tiny girl."

"Not so tiny now," James said in triumph. "Caro is quite a young lady these days. She will be home from school in time for Easter, and you will see her then. She is a very pretty creature, and quick-minded, like her poor mother. She speaks French and tinkles very pleasingly on the pianoforte, and her manners are most charming."

"We all dote upon her," Willow said softly. "But

you are staying? You are not going to rush away again soon?"

James looked at Nathan anxiously.

"If I had realized I would be so welcome, I'd not have stayed away so long," Nathan said drily.

"I had no wish to call you home before you were ready, or to bind you when it is a man's right to be free," James said earnestly.

"I am come home to stay," Nathan told him.

"Then we'll ride back to *Kingsmead* together—oh, but you came by stage!"

"Nathan can take my horse," Willow said sweetly.

"But won't you come up to the house with us?" Nathan asked.

"I have some sewing to do," Willow said, "and you and Uncle James will have a lot to discuss."

"Willow is eternally busy with her charities," James said. "Every orphan in the district has benefitted from her industry."

"I do what is necessary," Willow said with one of her shy, upward glances. "And nobody can ever persuade Aunt Eliza into church, so somebody has to set an example."

"Willow is an example to us all," James said when they had mounted and were riding back along the bridle path. "She would make someone a wonderful wife, but it is quite impossible to persuade her even to consider the notion. And neither she nor Aunt Eliza will move out of the cottage. It is sheer pride, of course. I sometimes think that pride is the real curse of the Falcons."

"My mother," Nathan began, and stopped, seeing his father's face harden, his lips set grimly.

"We will not speak of her," he said at last. "She

left of her own free will, and in thirteen years there has been no word from her."

"Might she not have gone back to the farm, back to Wales?" Nathan persisted.

"It's possible. I have never made enquiry," James said coldly.

"But surely—"

"She knows where I am. If she wishes to come back she will come," James said. "But I'll not go seeking her. And though I cannot order you, it would please me if you respected my wishes in the matter."

"As you say," Nathan said. The image of his energetic, brown-eyed mother faded before the memory of the gifts showered upon him through his schooldays, the present reality of the aging father who had tried so hard to give him freedom.

"Tell me the news of the village," he invited. "And the estate? Does the spring sowing go well? We have fine weather for it."

The cloud lifted and James began to talk, eagerly and knowledgeably, of the improvements he planned.

At the cottage Willow cleared away the dishes and put more wood on the fire. She liked to have the place to herself, to pretend that she was already mistress of the small property. It was not that she wished Aunt Eliza any harm. Indeed, she was quite fond of Aunt Eliza. She was fond of Uncle James, too, and would feel even more affectionate when she finally learned that he had decided to leave Paget Place as well as Wittle Farm to her. There were times when she feared that he intended to leave Paget Place to Caro Browning.

When Willow thought of Caro her mouth thinned and she looked every minute of her thirty years. The girl had no right to be alive at all. It was a quirk of chance that the girl had not died in the fire, but she had survived, and James treated her as if she were his own daughter instead of a charity bastard.

Then Willow's face softened into a smile. Nathan was home again, still unwed, eager to settle down and help his father with the management of the estate. And he admired her. She had seen the old affection leap into his eyes when she had greeted him.

For a moment something akin to love swept through her being. There was a quality essentially fresh and honorable about her cousin which called out something buried deep in her own nature. It would be pleasant to be loved by Nathan, to have his arms about her and his voice whispering sweetness in her ear. And suddenly she was determined to be a good wife to him, and the elegant mistress of *Kingsmead*.

Staring into the heart of the rekindled fire, she thought suddenly that it did not matter if her uncle left Paget Place to Caro or not. As Nathan's wife she would eventually own far more than the bastard brat. To her own bastardy she paid no mind. As a child everything had conspired to remind her of that fact, but now she never allowed herself to remember it at all.

Nathan's heart sank as they rode into the courtyard of *Kingsmead*. Even John's exclamation of surprised greeting and Betsy's shy curtsey could not fill up the spaces left by those who were gone. The house was as he remembered it, but all trace of his mother had vanished. Her belongings, which had once strewn the parlor, had been all cleared away, and the musky perfume she favored no longer excited the air.

"A drink first? Supper will probably be late if Cook celebrates your return with one of her tasty inventions," James said as they warmed their legs before the fire in the great hall. "You can recognize a sound claret when you are offered one, I trust?"

"It will make a welcome change after French and Spanish wines."

"Continental wines have no body," James agreed. "I travelled with my brother years ago, made the Grand Tour. I was wretchedly seasick, and longed to be back in Marie Regina. These days I go often to London on business in the Lords, but I enjoy it no more than I enjoyed the Grand Tour."

"You've made your mark in reform matters," Nathan said.

"One has to do something," James said wearily. "We weep over the plight of miners and chimney sweeps and millworkers, and rightly so. We forget that many farmworkers live in hovels and cannot afford meat from one year's end to the next, unless the squire hands out charity turkeys at Christmas. Most yeomen are as tied to the land as the medieval serfs were, and with as little prospect of advancement!"

"I cannot recall you ever grinding the faces of the poor," Nathan said, amused.

"But as a peer I have an opportunity, and a duty, to put my ideals into practice over a wider area. And my duty fills up the days." For a moment his face bore a listening look, as if he waited to hear the swishing of a skirt over the flagstones. Then he smiled and clapped Nathan on the shoulder, raising his voice into cheerfulness. "And now you are come home! I have often wished for this day, wished for it more than I can say. But you had to have your chance, my boy. That was my duty."

"I intend to stay," Nathan said.

"I'm glad of it," James said, and turned aside to blow his nose vigorously.

"Willow and Aunt Eliza will be glad of your company, too," he said after a moment. "Why, when Caro comes home we might even give a supper party. You would like that, wouldn't you? It would be quite a treat for Willow, too. The poor girl has very few pleasures."

"And Caro?"

"Caro will be the belle of the ball," James said affectionately. "She's a taking little creature. There will be no shortage of admirers for her in a year or two. Mind, I'd not have her snap up the first offer she receives. At her age she has the whole world ahead of her."

Chapter 14

"It looks desolate," Nathan said. "More desolate than I imagined it would be."

He gazed at the grass-grown spaces between the blackened shell of the manor house. The tangled briars of untended roses twined about the gaping entrance where the front door had been.

"Did you know that your father loved my mother once and prepared the manor for her?" Willow asked.

He nodded slowly, his eyes troubled. His mother had always disliked the very sound of Huldah Clegg's name, and gone out of her way to ignore Willow. But his mother was gone, unlikely ever to return.

"When I was small," Willow said, "I used to wonder how it would have been if my mother had married your father and I had been born here, instead of over at Wittle Farm."

"My father intends to leave Wittle Farm to you," Nathan said. "He told me about it."

"Because my grandfather was bailiff there, I know."

"It could make a pleasant home. There's a good piece of acreage with it."

197

"And you won't object? To have your property cut down?"

"Lord, no! The property is too large for one man anyway. Wittle Farm and, I suppose, the cottage for you when Aunt Eliza goes. And Paget Place for Caro. That still leaves more than enough for me."

"Did Uncle James say that he was going to leave Paget Place to Caro, then?" Willow asked.

"Didn't he tell you?"

"Oh, years ago he may have mentioned it, but I have no sense of property at all," Willow said lightly.

"Few women have, which is why men were put in the world to take care of them," Nathan said, taking her hand.

"Uncle James has always been most generous," she murmured.

"He felt Caro ought to be well provided for," Nathan said.

"Because of the way her mother died. It was a great tragedy," she nodded understandingly.

"And on the same night my mother rode away and never came back. On the same night."

"Only a day after that doctor left the village."

"Which doctor?"

"The one with gypsy blood. Dr. Evans, wasn't that his name?"

"I'd forgotten all about him," Nathan said.

"So had I, until this moment. Odd, wasn't it? Him going without a word, and then the manor burning down, and then Lady Mair—"

"The doctor was often up at the big house," Nathan said slowly, "and my mother was forever down in the village, in the house he rented from her. You don't think—"

"Oh, you must never think such a thing! For what—

ever reason she left, I'm certain that she loved your father. I'm certain of it." She had gripped both his hands and was gazing up intensely into his face.

"You're very sweet, Willow," he said gently. "Very sweet indeed, my cousin. I don't believe that you're capable of harboring an evil or malicious thought."

"It's all past now, anyway," she said. "Whatever happened, or didn't happen, is over now. Best to forget it, Nathan."

"And think about the supper party tomorrow," He kissed the tip of her nose and smiled at her. "I ought to start off for home now. Caro is arriving some time today, and I promised Father I'd be back to welcome her."

"He sent John over to meet her with the pony-trap, I suppose. He always frets if she travels by stage."

"He would fret if you went by stage, too," Nathan said.

"Oh, me! I never go anywhere!" She broke away, twirling lightly round in the unkempt grass, her coils of hair swinging loose, shining in the sun.

He watched her, fascinated by the movements of her small hands as they twined a pattern in the air. There was a wierd, brittle gaiety about her, unlike anything he had seen in a woman before. Impossible to realize that she was three years older than he, and already an old maid.

"Your hair's come down," he said at last, and she stopped dancing and put her hands up to her head, laughing through slitted, down-slanting lids.

"I sometimes forget that I'm a woman grown," she called out and sped away from him, twisting and turning down toward the river, the grass springing up behind her as she ran.

She probably expected him to follow. He wanted to

follow her, but the brooding ruin and the thoughts it had engendered stayed him. He watched her go, and then remounted his horse and rode slowly along the drive toward the main road again.

His father was in the great hall when he walked in. James's face had shed something of its grey, drained aspect, and his voice was cheerful.

"Caro is home! Come and see for yourself, Nathan. Our little Caro is home."

But she was not little. She was nearly as tall as her mother had been, and graceful as a wand in a full-skirted, balloon-sleeved dress of blue taffeta patterned with pink flowers and silvery leaves. Out of the silky, petal-edged collar her neck rose up like the stem of some exotic flower. Her black hair was piled in ringlets on her small head, and her blue eyes, their lashes sooty, fixed upon him with shy admiration.

"Caro? Little Caro Browning?" He took her narrow white hands in disbelief.

"I am older now than when you used to come up to the manor house and play with me," she said.

"Do you remember that?" he asked in surprise.

"You used to give me rides on your back," she said, and the dimple in her cheek grew deeper. "I can remember that very clearly, sir."

"You must call him Nathan," James said, "for he is like kin to you."

"The only kin I have are the Falcons," Caro said with a little, crooked smile that lent character to her flawless face. "And nobody could wish for a kinder family. Since my mother died, your father has been— like a father to me."

There was nothing in her to hint at her brutish begetting. In appearance she was the epitome of an aristocratic young lady, with something Gallic in the tilt of her head.

"And you have been a good daughter to me," James said. "Well, Nathan, what do you think of our little Caro now?"

"I think the age of miracles is not yet past," Nathan said teasingly, "for I remember her as a vast nuisance, forever running after me and demanding rides!"

"And now she is an educated young lady," James said proudly. "She plays the pianoforte beautifully, and her watercolors are charming."

"Will you play something for me?" Nathan asked.

"Later, when you have told me about all the exciting places you have visited." She bestowed upon him another dimpled, enchanting smile, and glided to the decanter to pour a drink for him. Over her shoulder she said, "I thought you would have been wed by now. Uncle James and I often wondered if you would come back one day with a beautiful foreign wife."

"I'd wager there's not a prettier girl than Caro in any corner of Europe," James said.

"She is exquisite," Nathan said, and, watching her over the rim of his glass, saw her blush hotly and then grow shyly pale again.

She retired early after supper, declaring that she was fatigued to the bone after her journey.

"And I shall sleep late tomorrow as if I were a grand lady," she said, "and in the afternoon Betsy shall do my hair in the new fashion, and I spent my quarter allowance on the sweetest gown you can imagine."

"Which you intend to wear at the supper party tomorrow."

"Of course, Uncle, and I shall dazzle all the neighbors. Are they all coming? The Stones, the Fiskes, Mr. Penn?"

"We will be thirty at table." James patted her cheek affectionately, but after she had run upstairs, his eyes returned broodingly to his son.

"Her background is a sad and sordid one," he mused. "I sometimes fear that, despite all her advantages, it will weigh against her in any possible match."

"Are people so intolerant?"

"Bastardy in an aristocrat is seldom accounted," his father said wryly. "But the daughter of a governess and a brute—people find that hard to forget. I hope she marries. I hope some man loves her sufficiently to overlook the circumstances of her birth."

"She is scarce sixteen," Nathan objected.

"I said that about Willow once," James said restlessly, "and now she is thirty and unlikely to wed. I recall, when I was a boy, people were saying much the same thing about Aunt Eliza. The years pass quickly."

"You do not enquire about my own marriage?"

"Because that is your own business, but I confess it would be pleasant to have grandchildren." James glanced at him hopefully. "Have you a lady in mind? You have not been home long enough to look about you."

"Would you mind if I wed?" Nathan enquired. "It would mean a new mistress for *Kingsmead*."

"A breath of life, you should say. New blood in the family; a chance to throw off the shackles of the past," James said with enthusiasm. "Come, you do have somebody in mind!"

"I was thinking of Caro," Nathan said.

"Caro? You would—but you have not seen her in years until tonight!"

"And I am no stranger to the charms of beautiful

young ladies." Nathan grinned suddenly. "You must not think I wasted my time in Europe on sightseeing round churches! I have even fancied myself in love once or twice, but when I saw Caro today—"

"You were caught by her charms and loved her to distraction all in a second."

"No, it is not as simple as that," Nathan said thoughtfully. "It was much more a recognition, a wanting to protect her, to—possess her, if you like. You spoke of intolerance, Father. How would you feel if Caro was to be married into our family?"

"I would be delighted," James said promptly. "Caro is not only my responsibility, but also my joy. In many ways, I think she has grown up as I would have wished Joan to grow up. To give her to you would secure her happiness, I believe."

"But I would not have you think I am going to leap into matrimony without making certain that Caro knows her own mind," Nathan said earnestly.

"No female knows her own mind," James said, "least of all a schoolgirl of sixteen. And Caro has a gentleness in her like her mother. I remember when I first engaged Felice Browning as a governess. She looked at me out of terrified blue eyes, clasping her hands together to stop their trembling. Your mother disliked her from the beginning. She resented the kindness I showed the poor girl, and yet in the end, I failed her. If I had accompanied her that evening she would not have been attacked. If I had not settled her in the manor house—no matter! So, you think of her daughter, do you? It would please me very greatly if you could persuade her to love you. She is ripe for it, my boy."

Like a cherry that hangs tenderly beneath its canopy of white blossom, Nathan thought. Or a star-shaped

flower hidden in a green bank. As Caro's image swam
into his mind he wished fervently that he had some
gift of poetry or painting so that he could capture the
sweetness of his vision and leave it for posterity to
see. The fleeting affairs he had enjoyed seemed, in
retrospect, cheap and shoddy.

Eliza, watching the guests move about in the great
hall, fanned herself energetically and decided she
enjoyed social affairs more than she had as a girl.
Not that there had been very many at *Kingsmead;*
her father had detested the idea that any of his
daughters might meet a man whom they could love.
And in the end, both Helen and Apple had run away
to be wed, and only she had remained the spinster
her father intended them all to be.

"Six of us," she said aloud, "and all dwindled
down."

"I beg your pardon, Miss Falcon. You were saying—"

She blinked in annoyance at the Vicar, who had
sat down beside her, a polite smile on his face.

"Six of us in the family once," she repeated. "And
only Prescott and Apple had children, and of the
marriage between James and Mair, only Nathan is
left. The Falcons will die out unless he makes haste
to marry. Perhaps that's not such a bad thing, eh?"

"Come, come, you cannot mean it, dear lady!" he
protested. "A splendid, ancient family such as your
own? Landed gentry, Miss Falcon. The backbone of
England."

"Did you know," she asked, snapping her fan shut,
"that my father was a possessive tyrant who drove my
mother to suicide? Did you know that my sisters had
to run away before they could marry the men they
loved, that my youngest brother was tricked into the

army, that Weston was so terrified of marriage that
he became—strange, twisted in his ways?"

"Every family has its little difficulties," the Vicar
said unhappily.

"As you say." She gave a bark of laughter and then,
taking pity on him, said, "And James is a fine, honorable man. Nathan, too. Good, healthy specimens, both
of them! I wish my nephew's marriage had turned
out more happily. That was a bad business." She
frowned as she spoke. Her imagined reconciliation
between James and Mair had been insubstantial as a
vapor.

"Miss Willow looks most pleasing this evening," Mr.
Penn observed.

Aunt Eliza's blue eyes flickered to where Willow
stood alone near the table. She was in pink, the short
sleeves and low neckline edged with gold, the full
skirt embroidered with diamonds and lozenges of
gold. A narrow scarf of pink gauze was tied about her
loops of pale hair.

"Willow is always pleasing," Eliza said. "Such a
queer creature she was as a child, forever wandering
off by herself, never playing with other children. But
affectionate, mind! There is a deal of affection in
Willow."

"And Miss Caro is quite the belle of the ball," Mr.
Penn said.

"Caro is beautiful," Eliza said. "Very like her mother. That dress she's wearing must have cost James a
pretty penny."

The dress, which had already excited the com-
ments of other lady guests, was modestly cut, but
ended daringly at the ankles. Of honey-colored
satin, it was looped with swathes of flowers in every
shade of spring. At each side of the high-curled chi-

gnon of hair, posies of flowers twined, falling at last to the long ringlets that touched her shoulders.

At her side Nathan strolled, his brown head bent, his eyes on her glowing young face. Her gloved white hand rested lightly on his arm, the satin of her skirt whispered against the pearl grey of his trousers.

"You have been most attentive to me, sir."

"Because I am enchanted, bound up in a spell and hoping never to break my bonds."

"Do you talk to all the ladies in such a fashion, sir?"

"Nathan. You must call me Nathan, for I am a kind of . . . adopted brother. Do you think of me as your brother, Caro?"

"Why, no, sir—Nathan."

"As my cousin, then? Do you think of me as your cousin, Caro?"

"It is very warm in here. My cheeks are burning."

"Then we will step out into the courtyard for a few minutes. The door is open, and the moon is rising."

They passed out into the moonlit courtyard, their fingers touching and entwining, their voices fading into whispers.

"I have always loved this house more than any house in the world," Caro said softly.

"It is your home."

"Because your father is the kindest, most generous man in the world."

"I, too, can be generous and kind."

"Oh, I know. It was not my intention to hurt your feelings," she said quickly.

"Dear Caro, you are incapable of hurting anybody's feelings," he said.

"Oh, I have quite a temper," she said proudly, treading across the cobbles toward the archway. "My teachers at school declare it is impossible to make me sit still for longer than ten minutes at a time."

"Do you like your school?"

"It's well enough," she said indifferently, "and, of course, I must be educated so that I may marry one day."

"Would you like to be married?" he enquired.

"I don't wish to be an old maid," she said, "but if I marry I will have to leave *Kingsmead*. I will have to go and live with my husband, you see."

"Unless your husband lived at *Kingsmead*, too."

"With Uncle James and—oh, I think I see." She put her hand to her mouth and stared at him.

"Do you see? Do you truly see?"

"I am—you only met me yesterday."

"I gave you rides on my back when I was a boy, and you were no more than three years old. You are hopelessly compromised."

"You are older than I am," she faltered.

"Eleven years is not such a tremendous gap," he argued.

"Oh, I cannot tell. I cannot tell what I ought to do," she said.

His arms were about her, crushing her to him, and all her doubts and fears were vanishing under the pressure of his mouth. "I have frightened you," he said, drawing away but holding her lightly. "I never meant to frighten you or hurt you, Caro."

"You could not frighten me," she said softly. "I waited for such a long time for you to come home again, and I thought about you so often that when you did come you didn't seem like a stranger."

"My father would be pleased to welcome you truly as his daughter."

"And I have no father." She made a small sound

between a sob and a laugh, and said again, "I have no father, Nathan. My mother was forced against her will."

"It is not important," he said, and kissed her again, tracing the outline of her ear and throat, hearing somewhere, vague as the wind's echo, a light step behind them.

"I would not disturb you for the world, cousin," Willow said, "but they are making up a set for the quadrille, and Miss Stone is going to play for us."

"Have you been there for long?" Nathan asked, a rare sharpness in his voice.

"A moment or two. If you wish to conduct your flirtations in secret you ought to choose a more private place."

"It is not a flirtation," Caro said. "You mustn't think badly of us."

"My love, it is none of my business," Willow said, amused.

"Nathan wishes to marry me," Caro said. "Is it not a great honor?"

"Is this true?" Willow asked. "Have you really decided to take a wife so soon after your return?"

"I have made up my mind to take the woman I love," Nathan said.

"Then Caro is a very fortunate girl. Is it to be announced tonight?" Willow asked.

"Lord, no! there are many things to be discussed. We have only just decided to wed," Nathan said.

"And I interrupted you! Forgive me for being where I am not wanted."

"But of course you are wanted!" Caro broke away from Nathan and put her arms about the older woman. "You have always been one of the people I love best, and you will be happy for me, won't you?"

"If you truly love each other," Willow said, returning the embrace, "then I do wish joy in your marriage."

"But it is a secret yet, mind," Caro warned.

"My lips are sealed." Willow put her fingers across her mouth. "But you must let me give you a bridal spray, at least!"

She darted to where the branches of the luck-tree spread themselves against the wall and snapped off a thin branch, handing it to Caro, her voice sweetly-bell-like as she said,

"I shall think of you constantly from now on. I shall think of both of you. Now hurry back, do! If not, your secret may become a common talking point before the evening is over!"

"She is very good," Caro said, looking after the retreating figure. "I would not have her think that I was behaving badly."

"And you mean to accept me? I have hurried you into a decision—"

"I want to marry you," she interrupted. "I think I've wanted to marry you ever since I was a tiny girl. All those years you were away I dreaded hearing that you'd taken a wife, and when you came back, you weren't like a stranger at all."

"Dear Caro." He leaned to embrace her, but the leafy branch impeded him, its leaves exuding the vinegary scent that was part of their mysterious, haunting quality. For some reason the perfume irritated him, and he thrust the leafy branch away and kissed her more harshly than he had intended.

"Are we to have cards?" Eliza was demanding. "If so, you may count me out. I never did get any pleasure from flinging squares of colored pasteboard about!"

"They are having a quadrille," Mr. Penn said. "Miss Stone is to play."

"In that case I shall remain here. That woman does not play the pianoforte, she tortures it to death. Willow! You ought not to wander outside without a pelisse."

"I never catch a cold," Willow said tranquilly. "I've been talking to Nathan and Caro. They make a handsome couple, don't you think? Good-evening, Mr. Penn. I have not had the opportunity of bringing in my contribution for the Jew's basket yet, I'm afraid."

"Do forget your charities for one evening," Eliza begged. "Go and join the dancing. Mr. Penn was only telling me that he looked forward to standing up with you."

"Indeed, yes. It would be a great privilege," Mr. Penn assured her.

"Do excuse us then, Aunt dear. Mr. Penn, shall we join the set?"

"You must be chilled after all," Eliza fretted. "You are shivering my dear. Positively shivering!"

Chapter 15

It was the first wedding at *Kingsmead* for nearly thirty years.

"Not that the last one turned out too well in the end," Eliza said. "Mair was always a jealous woman. She resented anybody who took James's attention away from her. And yet, it was she who finally left him. Do I have to wear this bonnet?"

"It suits you," Willow said calmly. "It makes you look distinguished and aristocratic."

"I was a handsome girl," Eliza said complacently. "If I'd chosen I could have found a husband. I don't mind admitting that if I'd met somebody kind who truly cared—but there! it wasn't meant."

"You and I are alike," Willow said. "I shall never marry either."

"I wondered sometimes when you and Nathan were boy and girl," said Eliza. "Oh, you're three years older then he is, and then he went away, but when I first heard he'd come back, I did wonder."

"I'm very fond of Nathan," Willow said crisply, "but I have no romantic notions about him, I assure you."

"It would never have done, anyway," Eliza said. "The Falcons have made too much of a habit of wedding their cousins. It's not healthy in cattle, too much in-breeding, and the same applies to human beings. I believe fresh blood will strengthen the stock."

"They are very much in love," Willow said. She spoke gently, almost indifferently.

"Pooh! at sixteen Caro is no more than a babe-in-arms, as much in love with *Kingsmead* as she is with Nathan." Eliza replied. "Do you think another bow of ribbon would set it off?"

"No. It's elegant as it is, if you refrain from pulling the brim over your eyes."

"I wish it wasn't May. 'Marry in May and rue the day.' They used to say that when I was a girl. Your gown is charming, Willow. That silvery color is very becoming."

"We are both beautiful," Willow said lightly. "Shall we start? It will be bad luck to arrive after the bride."

"James is to give her away. I think he is truly delighted about the match," Eliza said.

"We are all delighted," Willow said. "Caro has seemed like a sister to me for years. A younger sister."

It was, despite the month, a fine day for a wedding. The breeze was sweet-scented, the young hops green, the corn already tapped with gold. As they drove up to the church door, there was a ripple of comment from the crowd gathered outside. Most of the greetings were for Eliza, who was regarded as something of a character and whose nonattendance at church was considered a minor eccentricity. A few nodded in Willow's direction, but most of the villagers felt slightly ill-at-ease with Huldah Clegg's daughter, despite her numerous charities.

"A lovely day for a bride, ladies," Mr. Penn said,

as he ushered them down from the pony trap. "I understand the wedding trip is to be taken to Paris."

"Caro's mother was half-French," Eliza said.

"And next year we may be seeing another bride, eh, Miss Willow?"

"Not if I have any say in the matter," Willow said pleasantly. "Aunt, dear, put your bonnet straight."

Eliza gave the offending bonnet a bang and walked steadily down the aisle to the family pew. Once settled there she glanced about her critically, being accustomed to attend services only at weddings and funerals.

Mr. Penn had a penchant for ritual, a leaning which brought him into conflict with some of his parishioners, but of which Eliza approved. She liked the effect of flowers and vestments against the grey stone walls, and the thick clouds of incense that spiralled up from the brass censor.

The little church, built with stones from the despoiled monastery on the hill, had been the setting for many events in the history of the Falcons. Her own parents had been married here, nearly a hundred years before. She supposed that on that day her mother had been hopeful and happy, unable to look into the future and see the long years of tyranny that lay ahead.

The fiddler drew his bow across the strings, and the congregation rustled to its feet. The bride, demure in white taffeta with orange blossoms on her bonnet, drifted down toward the altar rail, one hand resting lightly on James's arm, the other holding a spray of honeysuckle. With her curls falling over her shoulders, Caro looked almost like a child. Her voice, making the responses, trembled on the edge of tears, and her

glance, as she looked at Nathan, pleaded for understanding.

So many brides, Eliza thought, and how many of
them are truly happy? There was an unaccustomed
film of moisture across her sharp blue eyes. She
tugged the brim of her bonnet further down, and
glared sideways, defying anybody to notice.

Willow watched the ceremony with dry eyes, her
hands lightly clasping the black stone. She drew
strength from the stone, feeling it vibrate between her
palms. They were singing "The Lord is my Shepherd."
Her own lips moved silently. "I shall not want. Nathan is mine. Nathan will be mine. Lilith, goddess of
the dark moon, put the means into my hands, and
bestow upon me the power to carry out my purpose.
Let him enjoy her for less than a year."

She was deeply fond of Nathan, and would not
grudge him a few months of romantic happiness with
the girl he believed he loved. He would quickly discover that Caro Browning was too young and too
shallow, but it would be better for him to find it out
for himself. Otherwise, he would spend the rest of
his life agonizing over a dream he had never possessed.

"He leadeth me beside the still waters. The river
runs high in the winter. It might be possible to lure
her down there. Look at that tiny fish, Caro, wriggling
between two stones! Look, Caro! Down there, pretty
Caro. But Caro was a strong swimmer. It was becoming fashionable for ladies to venture into the water.
Sweet Lilith, the river is not deep enough. We will
have to find another way, Lilith, you and I."

It's cold in the church, Caro thought. I hope that
I'm not going to catch a cold on my wedding day.
Nathan won't love me with a red nose and watery

eyes. I wish we were not going to Paris. All those years in school and as soon as I'm married I have to go away again. Three months, Nathan said, and that means we lose the best of the summer. It really is cold in here.

It might have been Joan, wedding a young man, James said to himself. Caro is like a daughter to me, doubly so now that she is marrying Nathan. He will be good to her, never remind her of her beginnings.

Nathan had nothing in his mind but the desire to protect the fragile creature with whom he had just exchanged vows.

The wedding breakfast was an elaborate one, with half the village invited, presents displayed on the tables in the drawing room, Betsy in a black silk gown to serve. Spring blossoms entwined the stone balustrade and filled the vases down the centre of the table. The time passed in a babble of conversation, of smiling toasts, of embarrassed speeches.

"John has brought the pony trap round to the courtyard. Are you ready, Caro? Nathan?"

They were all going to the door, crowding together, throwing rice. Caro, in a blue pelisse that matched her eyes, came down the stairs with Nathan's arm about her.

"You have been a good child," James said, as he kissed her cheek. "I've done my best for you. Now I entrust you to Nathan."

A flash of slender ankles as she climbed up into the trap, and Caro had turned and was throwing her bouquet of honeysuckle into the crowd.

"Willow has caught it!" Eliza cried.

"So Miss Willow may be walking down the aisle as I predicted," Mr. Penn beamed.

Willow held the flowers almost at arms' length, her

face expressionless. She had reached up instinctively to catch the bouquet, and now she stood perfectly still, the honeysuckle yellow against the silvery-grey of her gown. Then a smile curved her pale lips, and she bowed her head slightly as if to hide it.

With Nathan and Caro gone, *Kingsmead* settled down to its accustomed summer round. Looking back later, Willow could not remember a more luxuriant summer. Cloudless day followed couldless day, and the occasional rainy evening served only to enhance the glitter of bough and blossom. The harvest spread itself under the sky in a promise of prosperity for the winter.

"We will have the long bedroom fitted out as a sitting-room for Caro," James said. "She will like that."

The long bedroom was above the drawing room, being part of the wing added in the seventeenth century by old Nathaniel Paget, who had married the notorious Regina Falcon. Eliza and her sisters Helen and Apple had slept there as girls.

"May I help with the room?" Willow asked. "It will be such a pleasant surprise for Caro when she and Nathan get back."

She worked hard during the summer, going into Maidstone to choose hangings and carpets, harrying the decorators until they had mixed their paint to the exact shade she required, insisting that a wood engraver be hired from London to chisel tiny, mocking faces on the cornices of the high ceiling.

"Very pretty, indeed," Eliza said, puffing slightly after her ascent of the stairs. "This has cost a pretty penny, I'll be bound."

"Uncle James assured me that expense was no object," Willow said.

"And you took him at his word, didn't you?" Eliza

leaned on the stick she had reluctantly begun to carry and let her eyes roam around the panelled walls of pale grey, the carpet patterned in a design of twisting silver and green leaves, the hangings of pearl, the bowls of dried grasses.

"Very pretty," she said again. "The room reflects you, Willow. Upon my soul, you might have designed it for your own use!"

"It is for Caro," Willow said, and again the little secret smile appeared on her lips.

They came home in September, when the moon hung low over the mellow acres and the starlings fanned out in mystic triangles across the sky. James insisted that Eliza and Willow should come to supper to welcome back the honeymoon couple. The prospect of their return had put a fresh spring in his step, and his face had lost some of its haggard aspect. When the pony trap rattled into the courtyard, he was on his feet at once, his expression eager, his voice hearty as he strode to the door.

"Caro! Nathan! Come in out of the cold. These night breezes can be very treacherous for ladies. Such a long journey you must have had! Were you very sick on the crossing?"

"The Channel was calm as a millpond, Father. Even Caro found no discomfort in the motion of the vessel," Nathan said.

"Even Caro, indeed! I am an excellent sailor," Caro said indignantly.

They were coming into the great hall. Caro's slim frame was wrapped in a fur-trimmed cape; her small face was haloed in white fur. Her blue eyes were as bright as her cheeks.

"Honeymoons evidently agree with you," Eliza said, coming to embrace her.

"Honeymoons with Nathan do," Caro said, sparkling. "Oh, we had a splendid time, Uncle James! I cannot understand why you didn't enjoy your Grand Tour when you were a boy. Paris is a lovely city, Uncle! I never saw so many fine paintings or such grand buildings in my life. Oh, we learned something of them at school, but actually seeing them is an entirely different matter. And Nathan explains everything so beautifully."

As if he were the teacher and she the pupil, Willow thought, watching as Caro peeled off cloak and hood. In the younger girl's voice there was no echo of remembered passion. Her eyes were innocent. Yet she must have lain in Nathan's arms, returned his embrace, known the warmth of his flesh.

"Willow has a surprise for you," James said. "Willow, take Caro upstairs and show her, you know."

As if she were a little girl who must have gifts wrapped up for her, thought Willow. Aloud she said, "Yes, do come upstairs and see, Caro. It's more Uncle's idea than mine, though, and he paid for it all."

"A drop of port, my boy," James was saying, as the two women went up the stairs.

"Some of that port for me, too, if you please," Eliza interrupted.

"Port is not a fashionable drink for ladies," Nathan said.

"Then thank the Lord I'm not a fashionable lady," Eliza said briskly. "Make it a respectable drink, James, enough to taste. You should make Caro drink port, Nathan. She has a fine-drawn look about her."

"Nonsense! She's as healthy as any woman I've ever met," James said. "She never ailed even as a child, apart from nightmares. Do you remember the nightmares she used to have, Aunt Eliza? She grew out of them when she went to school."

In the newly furnished and painted sitting room Caro gazed about her with clasped hands.

"But it's divine!" she breathed. "Did you choose all these things by yourself? How clever of you!"

"You like it, then?"

"Like it! Dearest Willow, it's heavenly. I never could have matched up shades so beautifully! It's like being inside a seashell, isn't it?"

Caro put her arms around Willow and hugged her. She smelt of lavender and Willow, disliking the fragrance and disliking still more the bodily contact, drew away.

"I shall be able to have sewing parties here," Caro said. "Not that I enjoy sewing very much, but I do like to gossip. At school, after the lights were put out, we used to gather on one bed and invent scandalous stories about the mistresses."

"It must have been vastly amusing," Willow said.

"Oh, it didn't stop me from feeling homesick," Caro said earnestly. "Even when we were in Paris I kept looking forward to coming back to *Kingsmead*. Oh, I intend to be a perfectly splendid wife for Nathan."

"I'm sure you do," Willow said.

"He's really very kind to me," Caro said. "I was a little nervous that he might think me too young, but he says I make him laugh with my foolishness. And I am determined to be a good wife to him. Listen! I'll tell you a secret, one that not even Nathan knows yet. Can you keep a secret, Willow?"

"Yes, of course."

"There's to be a baby," Caro said, her voice a conspiratorial whisper. "I'm going to have a baby, Willow."

"Are you certain of it?" was all that Willow could find to say.

"Oh, I'm quite certain," Caro assured her. "It will be born next March, or perhaps early April—I'm not absolutely sure about that."

"I see." Willow went over to the long window and stood, looking out across the purpling lawns. At their farthest edge were the dark shapes of trees where the deer park bounded the property, and beyond the trees lay the open heath where the gypsies had once camped every summer. It had been on a night such as this that Felice Browning had set out to go to church, and now, sixteen years later, her bastard stood calmly in the beautiful room, secure in her position as Nathan's wife and the future Lady Falcon—

"Do you want the child?" Willow asked.

"Want it? Why, everybody wants babies, don't they?" Caro asked.

"Not unless they have husbands," Willow said drily. "You and I, my dear Caro, cannot pretend to ourselves that we were ever wanted."

"But Aunt Eliza has always treated you as if you were her own child," Caro said, looking troubled, "and nobody could have been kinder than Uncle James has been to me. We have both been very fortunate all our lives."

"Yes, of course. We must always be grateful," Willow agreed.

"And you will be the baby's godmother, won't you?" Caro begged prettily. "If it is a girl we could call her Willow, if you like."

"That's very kind of you."

As they turned to go, Willow could not resist asking, "Have you never thought evil of anybody?"

"Why should I? I never met anyone who was evil," Caro said.

"Not even Lady Mair?"

"We can't be certain she really did what we think she did," Caro said, "and if she did, why, that shows she must have been very unhappy, doesn't it? I think evil people must always be very unhappy, don't you? Shall we go downstairs? And you won't say anything, will you? I want to tell Nathan myself later tonight!"

Again there was the sweetness of lavender, the suffocating hug of white arms. Then Caro whirled out to the gallery and her voice rang gaily down the stairs.

"Uncle James, the room is superb! Nathan, you must come and see the lovely sitting room that I have, and Willow has chosen the furnishings so cleverly. Dearest, where is the bag with the presents in it? We bought gifts in Paris. Some beautiful lace for you, Aunt Eliza, and a set of hunting prints for you, Uncle, and a dear little clock for Willow."

A clock to tick away the waiting hours until this ridiculous marriage is over. And there is going to be a child. An heir for *Kingsmead*. It might have been my child, Willow said to her reflection in the glass. It might have been mine, if Nathan hadn't lost his senses and rushed into marriage with a pretty doll.

Staring at her own face, greenish in the subtle colors of the room, she was honest enough to admit that she had never really craved a child of her own. The prospect of growing heavy and unwieldy like the village women she had seen, of enduring long hours of pain and the violation of her privacy, was not appealing.

But it would be interesting to rear a child, to cause it to love her, to smooth its path in life. The opportunity lay in her own hands, if she cared to take it.

She smiled into the glass, proud of her smooth skin and heavy hair. In ten years Caro's china-doll prettiness would have faded, and Willow and she would look much of an age. But in ten years time Caro would be mouldering bones, like poor Uncle Weston and the gypsy woman.

"Nathan looks well, doesn't he?" Eliza remarked as they drove home. "Marriage evidently agrees with him, and James has shed years since the two of them came home. Do you know, it wouldn't surprise me in the least if Caro were already pregnant? I always did have an eye for such things."

"Did you, indeed?" Willow held the reins capably, guiding the pony onto the main road.

"A baby at *Kingsmead* would be pleasant," Eliza said. "I always did like babies, puppies, kittens, all young things. They're a sign that God has not despaired of the world. Caro struck me as looking a mite feverish."

"Perhaps she was weary after the journey," Willow said cautiously.

"A girl of sixteen has no business to be weary," Eliza said firmly. "At her age I had more energy than any of my brothers."

"She was, perhaps, a trifle drawn," Willow said.

"Her blood is thin," Eliza said. "You must make up one of your mixtures for her, Willow."

"If you think it will do any good," Willow said.

They had turned down the bridle path, the wheels of the trap scarcely fitting between the trees. It required a skillful hand to guide the vehicle along the rutted earth. As they drew up in the clearing, Eliza proclaimed with satisfaction, "All safe, all sound! It's good to get back to the Dower Cottage. I was born and reared in the big house, but I'd not return there now."

"Is it really true that the witch who cursed the Falcons lived at this cottage?" Willow asked.

"So they say."

"And what did she look like?"

"Who knows? There was never a portrait painted of her, only of her daughter. I think she may have been red-haired."

"Black-haired," said Willow. "I think she was black-haired, and her eyes were yellow, like the eyes of a cat or a fox. And she was tiny, like me."

"You talk as if you knew her personally," Eliza said, clambering to the ground.

"I was imagining. That's all. Be careful you don't trip up over your dress."

"I'm not in the habit of tripping up," Eliza said crossly. "You must not treat me as if I were in my dotage."

"You are the youngest woman in the world," Willow said. "Let me open the door for you. There! I'll stable the pony and then come in and build up the fire. Would you like a nice hot mug of punch before we go to bed?"

"On top of port and that wine James served us at supper?" Eliza laughed, displaying still-excellent teeth. "Why not? It will be cozy together, just the two of us."

"Just the two of us," Willow said.

At this moment Uncle James would be sitting by the fire in the long drawing room, a glass of whisky by his side, an expression of contentment on his face because his beloved Nathan and his equally beloved Caro were at *Kingsmead* again.

And Nathan and Caro would be together, perhaps in the sitting room that Willow had designed. More probably they were in the bedroom, clasping hands in the big, curtained bed. She could see them as clearly as if she were there, and hear Caro's soft whisper.

"Oh, Nathan, I have a secret to tell you. You will never guess what it is, darling. Or perhaps you will guess. You would like a baby, wouldn't you, dear heart?"

And Nathan, his blue eyes dark with dreaming, turning to put his arms around her, to hold her tenderly, to promise her the earth if she bore him a healthy child.

"Do close the door, Willow," Eliza said testily. "There's quite a breeze blowing up from the river tonight. After such a glorious summer the winter may be a harsh one."

"There's frost on the moon tonight," Willow said. Above the trees the moon glittered and shone and dissolved into dew. With surprise Willow felt the cold, slow trickle of tears on her face.

It was against all the rules. The dark daughters of Lilith were not permitted the weakness of tears. But the drops went on sliding down her cheeks all the while she was unhitching the pony.

Chapter 16

"Two months more to go, and I'm so bored I could die." Caro's small face was puckered in a discontented frown and she moved restlessly, pleating the voluminous skirt of her loose dress.

"The last two months are always the worst," Willow said.

"How could you possibly know? You've never had a baby," Caro said crossly.

"That's true. I have no right to make any pronouncements on the subject."

"Dear Willow, I'm sorry!" Caro leaned impulsively to embrace the older woman. "I never meant to speak so sharply, but I'm in a horrid humor today. And with Uncle James and Nathan both in London—it was too bad of them both to go!"

"Uncle James had business in the Lords—"

"And Nathan is there to sit on the new Poor Relief Committee. I know, I know. But why do they have to choose this particular month? I hate January, with Christmas over and the spring too far off."

"But it's a beautiful day," Willow said, laying aside

her sewing. "The world is white and crisp, and there is scarcely a breath of wind. It would do you a great deal of good to go out for a while."

"I can't walk far without getting tired," Caro complained.

"We could take the pony trap. I'd drive very slowly and carefully, so you wouldn't be jolted."

"I might catch a chill. You know I've had one cold after another all winter."

"You can wrap up warm and snug in the new pelisse that Nathan gave you for Christmas."

"It is pretty, isn't it?" Caro looked more cheerful. "But I'm so enormous, Willow! Folks see me coming long before my head's in view!"

"My, but you do have a fit of the dismals!" Willow exclaimed. "I'll tell John to hitch up the pony, and we'll take a drive down to the river. It's all frozen over now and looks charming. Come, put on your pelisse and your pattens. I'll help you strap them on. We can perhaps gather some holly sprays. They would look handsome on the supper table."

Fifteen minutes later the two of them were jogging down the drive. The main road had been cleared, the snow piled up along the ditches, small stones and grit thrown across the thin film of new ice. The trees were heavy with their burden of icicles, and in the meadows the stubble of corn and hay was white-frosted.

"It was good of you to come and sit with me today," Caro said, her face grateful and pleading as if she sought to amend her previous ill-humor. "Ever since I was little people have been good to me. You, and Aunt Eliza, and Uncle James, who treats me as if I were his own daughter."

"Yes."

"And now the babe will be his first grandchild. I intend to have a big family while I'm still young enough to enjoy them. At least four children—don't you think that's a nice even number?"

"Have one first," Willow said shortly. "The bridle path has been salted. Would you like to walk a little? You can take my arm."

She was looping the reins over the pony's back and climbing down as she spoke. Caro followed less nimbly, clutching at Willow's arm as she balanced on the wooden pattens.

"Shall we visit Aunt Eliza?" she enquired.

"Better not. Aunt Eliza always naps in the afternoons, though she'd be furious if anyone caught her at it. Let's walk among the trees, down to the river."

They moved slowly, two dark-clad figures in bonnets and pelisses, the taller leaning upon the smaller, slighter one.

"Doesn't it look pretty!" Willow cried, as they reached the bank. "In places the ice is so thin that you can see the dark water beneath. It's very cold under the ice, I should think. Cold as death."

"But when the spring comes the ice will melt," Caro said.

"So it will. Isn't that odd?"

"Why, what's odd about it?" Caro stopped and looked down at Willow.

"Oh, that some things are certain and others not certain at all," Willow said. "It's absolutely certain that the ice will melt, but by no means certain that either of us will be here to see it."

"There's no reason why we shouldn't be," Caro said.

"No reason in the world. Take no notice of me. I think I have the dismals myself," Willow said lightly.

"Worrying about Aunt Eliza and then worrying about—"

"About me? But you said having a baby would be easy, that there was no danger."

"No danger at all! At least, scarcely any that a healthy girl need bother about. And you are really quite strong, aren't you? Oh, the occasional chill, flush of fever, that's nothing at all. I am sure of it."

"But I have not been well for months," Caro said nervously. "You know how sick I've been ever since Nathan and I came home from Paris! I've taken all the mixtures you've given me, but they make me feel sick. They spoil my appetite, Willow."

"You will feel better when the baby comes."

"Will I? Sometimes I think—don't laugh at me, but sometimes I think I won't live to see the baby grow up," Caro said in a low voice.

"Do you really think so?" Willow looked concerned. "Do you really have some kind of premonition."

"I have bad dreams," said Caro. "I have a nightmare, and I don't know why, or what it means."

"What sort of dreams?"

"The same one. Always the same one." Caro twisted her hands together. "I am by a window, looking out into the darkness. I can hear a horse galloping and then I see the horse, with two figures on its back. And one of the figures falls down. And I beat on the window, but nobody hears me, and the darkness is all round me. You're very pale, Willow. Is something wrong?"

"A goose walking over my grave," Willow said.

"But isn't it strange, to have such a terrible dream night after night? And to have this feeling in me?"

"I think you ought to put it right out of your mind."

"But I can't." The girl's blue eyes had a lost, bewildered look. "I was so happy to come home from school, so happy when Nathan asked me to marry him. Yet I can't look ahead, Willow. I can't seem to make plans for after the babe is born. There is nothing there but darkness. You know, I have never imagined myself looking after the child or teaching it how to walk. If anything did happen, would you—"

"Care for the babe? Of course I would, but nothing is going to happen to you," Willow said swiftly.

"I wrote something the other day," Caro said, fumbling in her pocket. "It's a poem. Not a very good one, I'm afraid, but I wrote it down. If anything did happen, would you give it to Nathan?"

Her round, childish hand was clear on the sheet of paper. Willow read the words silently, her lips drawn in, her gaze hooded.

> If you go first, will you wait for me
> In the land where there is no time?
> Will you keep faith with the vow we vowed
> And still be mine?
> If I go first, will you follow me?
> Swift and sure and believing still?
> Never turn back and leave me there
> On the darkling hill?
> Seedtime was short and the harvest late
> And winter has frozen the swallow's lament,
> But the words I spoke as you entered my gate
> Were truly meant.

"Will you give it to Nathan?" Caro asked again. "Promise me."

"If you wish, but there'll be no need," Willow said. "These fancies you have are no more than that, just fancies. You will laugh at your own foolishness after the babe is born."

"Perhaps." Caro's face bore a strange look, as if some echo from the future reached her mind. "I'm very grateful to you, Willow. You've been a good friend to Nathan and me. Do you know, before he went to London, Nathan said to me, We must make shift to find a husband for good old Willow."

Rage such as she had not known since Mair had flung the stone that killed Beau flooded Willow's being. Red mist surrounded her, and in its midst Caro's silly doll face stared at her. Good old Willow. Must find her a husband. Good old Willow.

There was the splintering of ice, and a crashing of water, and Caro screaming. Somebody else was calling out from behind her among the trees. "What's happening? Who is making that terrible noise?"

Willow slithered down the frozen bank and grabbed at the long black curls that floated on the surface of the widening water. Desperation lent her strength, and then Eliza was at her side, helping to drag the sodden, inert bundle free from the swirling current.

"What happened? I was in the clearing when I heard the screaming. What happened?" Eliza was demanding.

"She was leaning forward to look at the ice," Willow said shiveringly. "She must have over-balanced. I couldn't stop her."

"You might have been drowned yourself," Eliza said accusingly.

"Is Caro—"

"Still alive, but her pulse is weak. You'd best run for Mistress Fiske and a couple of the men. She's too heavy for us to lift."

Eliza was sponging ice from the blue-white face.

Willow picked up her skirts and ran. Water dripped from her hair and clothing, and her breath was steam in the air.

"Lilith, forgive me! Forgive me for my stupidity. All these patient months, undermining her strength, making it harder for her to digest her food, to survive the ordeal of childbirth. And now my own temper puts the child at risk, two months too soon. Lilith, I want that baby! Let Caro die, but save the child."

Eliza was massaging Caro's wrists when Willow returned, running like a hare, with Mistress Fiske and three of the farm laborers panting behind.

"Lord have mercy! The poor soul! The poor soul!" Mistress Fiske began to wring her hands.

"You'd better carry her to the cottage." Eliza struggled to her feet and began to issue orders. "You'd best take the pony and ride to Maidstone, Jem. Get a physician. If you can find two, bring them both. We will have to build up the fire and boil some water and put clean linen on the bed. Willow, you ought to change at once! You are dripping all over everything, my dear child."

"I'll go on ahead, Aunt Eliza," Willow said obediently. Lilith, don't let the child die. Save the child, sweet Lilith!

The Dower Cottage was all bustle and running feet and comings and goings, punctuated by the thin, ragged cries of the girl in labor.

"Two months premature and the cord twisted!" Mistress Fiske said in despair. "And the poor child has no strength. Has someone sent for Lord Falcon and Master Nathan?"

"I told one of the men to send John to London. No point in waiting for the stage. As it is, it'll be morning before he reaches them."

Eliza pulled her mobcap straight and frowned distractedly about her. The excitement of the rescue, the tension of waiting, had roused in her much of her former youthful energy. But the strain was taking its toll, and for a moment she felt strongly inclined to sit down in the rocking chair and weep.

"Willow, if you've changed your dress, will you brew some rosemary tea?" she asked, blinking rapidly to dispell the threatened tears. "I'll try and make Caro swallow some. It will ease the pains."

"She is conscious, then?" Willow looked up.

"She would scarcely be making that dreadful noise if she were not," Mistress Fiske said tartly. "Poor little soul!"

"Has she said anything?" Willow asked.

"Not a word that makes sense. Too badly shocked," Eliza said wearily.

"I'd best go up to her again. She'll need to start bearing down soon, doctor or no doctor!" Mistress Fiske said, heaving her bulk up the narrow stairs. She had helped many folk into the world and laid them out, too, at the end, but in her sixty-three years she had never been faced with a half-drowned, half-frozen girl about to give birth two months before her time. She was by no means certain that her skill would be sufficient, and mingled with her genuine concern for the poor young lady was fear for her professional reputation.

"I'll come with you," Aunt Eliza offered, but her voice quavered and the fine old hand clutching the stick trembled violently.

"Sit by the fire. I'll help Mistress Fiske until the physician arrives," Willow said. Sweet Lilith, don't let Caro say anything. Don't tell them that I pushed you, Caro. It was a stupid, ill-judged action. An unnecessary thing to do. Keep the child safe, Lilith, but let her die in silence.

Night closed in around the cottage. Jem returned with the physician. Eliza dozed by the fire and woke with a sour taste in her mouth. The stars flickered under a cold moon.

"Miss Falcon?" The physician was tapping her on the shoulder as she gazed up at him, blear-eyed, chilly despite her shawl.

"Has something—is there news?" she asked.

"A boy, Miss Falcon. An heir for Mr. Nathan."

"Alive?"

"Alive, but small. Very small." The physician shook his head and rubbed his hands together. "But the child will live, I believe."

"And Caro?"

"Resting. Badly shocked and a great loss of blood. Much depends now on the next few hours. Inner resources of strength. Will to live. Miss Willow is sitting with her. I sent Mistress Fiske home to bed, and I advise you to do the same."

"I must look in on the child first. My great-great-nephew. Fancy that, now!"

Eliza looked greatly pleased at the notion.

"You'll have something to drink before you leave? Or will you be staying here?"

"I'll take a room at the inn," the doctor said, shrugging into his cape. "If there is any change, please send at once for me. The young lady is not strong. I fear. I assume that milord has been summoned?"

"Someone has set out for the city. Thank you for your help, doctor."

"These fine-boned females do not deliver well," the physician said gloomily. "Good-night to you, Miss Falcon."

She straightened herself with an effort of will, for she was tired and her bones ached, and mounted the stairs slowly.

Caro was laid on Willow's bed, her body flat beneath the coverlet, her face so white that it looked blue-shadowed, her black curls lank. Willow sat on a stool by the bed, her light eyes fixed on Caro, her small hands clasped loosely. A shallow linen chest in the corner held a mound of blankets shrouded closely around a tiny form.

Eliza narrowed her eyes to bring the small face into focus. She used her spectacles as seldom as possible, regarding the myopia of advancing age as a sign of weakness.

"He's like Nathan," she pronounced. "Not a trace of poor Caro. Is she asleep?"

Willow put her finger to her lips and shook her head.

"Call me if you need anything," Eliza said in a stage whisper, and tiptoed out. She was too tired to lace her stays, so she lay down on her bed as she was, and fell instantly asleep.

So that is childbirth, Willow thought, and shuddered. It had been pain and blood and humiliation, if Caro had been sufficiently aware to realize what was happening to her. Not for anything in the world would Willow ever allow such a thing to happen to her. Not even for Nathan could she endure such an experience.

Caro stirred and opened her eyes. The blue of them was clouded and the corners of her mouth twitched.

"You are like a sweet little wax doll," Willow said softly. "One might be tempted to stick pins in you, my dear."

Caro's face changed and quivered, the blurred eyes

widening with terror. One hand fluttered up and sank down again.

"Silly Carol I was only funning," Willow said gently.

"I was in the river," Caro whispered. Her voice was so low that the other had to bend to hear.

"You fell," Willow said. "You fell, Caro, and I pulled you out of the water. I did what I could, my dear."

"The baby—?"

Sweet Lilith, if she sees the child she will do everything in her power to remain alive. "Don't think about the baby now," Willow said.

"But I heard it cry."

"Best you don't see it until you are stronger," Willow soothed.

"Is something wrong with my baby?" Caro was gasping, striving to pull herself into a sitting position.

"You must try to understand," Willow's hands were silk, her voice honey. "Sometimes a babe is not very well. That happens when its parents are closely related."

"Related? I don't understand," Caro said faintly.

"God forgive me. I hoped you would never have to know," Willow said.

"Know what?" Caro's whisper was as frightened as her eyes. "*Know what?*"

"That Uncle James is your father."

"He's Nathan's father," Caro said.

"Your father, too. It's an open secret," Willow said. "That was why Lady Mair burned down the manor house and left. That was why Uncle James took you to *Kingsmead* and reared you and sent you to scoool. There never was any man who attacked your mother in the wood. It was Uncle James."

"I don't believe you." Scarlet patches of color

flamed in her cheeks and as suddenly drained away again.

"Dear Caro, you must never tell Nathan. He doesn't know," Willow said gently.

"Uncle James is my father?" Caro closed her eyes briefly. When she opened them again they had lost their dazed look and were bleak with despair. Yet her voice was stronger and more adult than Willow had ever heard it.

"Give Nathan the poem. Tell him that I loved him."

"Yes, of course."

"And take care of the babe. It's not his fault." Her voice was fading; she was shrinking down into a lifeless figure, with no color in eyes or skin, the blackness of her curls a mourning frame for blue-tinged lips and sharp, jutting nose.

Willow sat very still and watched life ebbing away, borne out upon the tide of shame and grief.

Caro died quietly, with a kind of pathetic dignity, as if all her young life had been spent in preparation for this moment. In those last breaths that trembled into the air there was all the acceptance of an aristocrat.

The false light that heralds the dawn was silvering the woods when Willow opened the shutters. She felt hot and sticky, but triumph was rising up in her. The babe was alive. Tiny, but perfect and living. She had bent over the linen chest and touched the curving cheek. A boy-child for *Kingsmead*. Nathan's child.

Riders were galloping into the clearing. She drew back from the window and sat down again, bowing her head, letting the tears slide down onto her hands. There were footsteps on the stairs and voices below, and then Nathan, travel-grimed and haggard, burst in.

"We had started for home when John met us on the road—is Caro? Caro?"

He stared from the bed to the chair, his face convulsed, and burst into a passion of tears. In the doorway behind them James stood, shoulders slumped, eyes brimming.

It was Nathan who spoke first, his voice slurred and thick. "What happened? Aunt Eliza said—for God's sake, what happened?"

"It was my fault," Willow sobbed. "We went for a walk by the river. Caro wanted to see it all frozen over. She slipped and fell through the ice. I managed to drag her clear, but the cold and the shock—I shall never forgive myself for allowing her to go. It was all my fault."

"Willow, dear Willow!" James came and put his arms about her. "You must never think such a thing, let alone give voice to it! John gave us some account of what happened. You risked your own life to save her. You can be proud of that.

"I loved her," Nathan said brokenly. "I loved her so much."

"She didn't have the strength," Willow said, rubbing her eyelids childishly with her knuckles. "The ordeal was too much for her. But you have a fine baby son, Nathan. He's very tiny because he came too soon, but he's sturdy."

"I don't want to see him." Nathan sank to his knees and buried his face in the coverlet.

"My first grandchild." James went over to the linen chest and looked down into the cocoon of blankets. His face was a mixture of grief and pride.

"She was so pleased to have a son," Willow said. "So proud."

"Poor Caro! Poor little girl," James said heavily. "Where's Aunt Eliza?"

"Still asleep, I suppose. She was worn out."

"I'd better break the news to her," James said. "She was very fond of Caro."

"I loved her," Nathan said, raising his head. "She was gay and pretty and full of life, and we loved each other. We loved each other and now she's dead. She was alive and now she's dead."

"Nathan, I'm so sorry, so desperately sorry." Willow rested her hand on his shoulder. In the half light her expression was serene and tender.

"Did she ask for me? Did she say anything before—" Nathan's voice broke.

"My dear, I'm so sorry."

"Not even a word? One word?"

"She said nothing," Willow said sadly. "She only asked me to take care of the babe. I'm so sorry, Nathan dear."

Epilogue

"And this year I am fifty years old," Mair said.

"Fifty indeed! And you not looking one day over twenty-five," said Huw Postman Bach.

"Go on with you! Get home to your wife before she has me thrown back over the border as a scarlet woman!"

"If you were I'd be running after you," Huw Postman Bach said gallantly.

His bullet head reached only to Mair's shoulder and he was far too much in awe of his even more diminutive wife to glance sideways at any other female, but the same comedy was played out between them every week.

"Wish I had a bit of post for you, Mrs. Price," he said now.

"What would I be doing with a letter?" Mair asked, smiling. "I've not a relative living to write to me."

"I'll write you a letter myself one of these days," he said stoutly. "Full of love-longing it will be. Full of the opportunities I lost through wedding too young. See you next week, Mrs. Price." He clambered back to the saddle of his pony and raised a hand in cheerful salute.

"Nice woman," he would tell Myfanwy later when they sat at supper. "Keeps herself to herself. Strict with her girls, mind. Very strict."

"It does no harm to be strict with girls," Myfanwy said, carving slices of ham to left and right. "Women are weak, nearly as weak as men."

"And in all the years since she came here, not a single letter. Not one visitor."

"It's my belief," said Myfanwy, spooning gravy, "that her husband was cruel to her, and she ran away, and took back her maiden name. The farm was in her family years ago, they tell me."

"Perhaps she never married at all," he hinted. Myfanwy's face brightened at the prospect of scandal, and then fell.

"Too respectable," she said judiciously. "I can pick out a bad woman at a hundred paces, but Mrs. Price has been married. I will swear to that. In chapel, if need be."

As Huw Postman Bach jogged down the track, Mair allowed herself a brief moment of sadness. Thirteen years without one word. Thirteen years of hoping for a letter, of praying that one day James would ride into the village, up to the farm, into the yard. She wiped her hands down the sides of her red skirt and went back into the house.

The stone building with its large living room and two smaller bedrooms had been rebuilt by her own parents from the stones of the original farmhouse. That had been before her birth, when her mother Apple Falcon had eloped with the artist Geraint Price. Mair had been born at Saron and had grown up there, learning from her mother the skills of a housewife, helping her father to work the land. She had buried them side by side after their deaths, and had travelled alone into Kent, where she had met and married her cousin.

Now her life had run full circle, and she was back in the place where she had begun. It had not been easy. If she could only go back through time she would behave so differently—or would she? Was it true that people trod a predestined road with no hope of escaping what lay at the end?

She pressed her lips tightly together and went inside the house. It was as sparsely furnished as when her parents had lived there, but with none of the gay, feminine touches that Apple Falcon had loved. A thread-bare rug covered the stone-flagged floor and the windows lacked curtains. A table with stools and a high-backed chair, a dresser and a grandfather clock were the only items of furniture in the apartment. Everything was scrubbed clean and neatly mended, the fire laid ready for lighting, the lamp trimmed. Against one wall hung a small mirror. She went over to it and stared intently at her face.

Huw Postman Bach had lied. She looked every minute of her fifty years. Her skin was roughened and reddened, after years of toil, her chestnut hair was almost completely grey, pouches of dark flesh blurred her jawline. She had put on a good deal of weight despite the frequent exercise she took. There was nothing left now of the boldly handsome woman who had loved James Falcon with such passion, who hungered so fiercely after Guto Evans.

She turned away, pressing her lips more tightly together as she heard her daughters running across the field. Not for worlds could she ever have admitted that she adored the twins. It did no good to show people they were loved. When one displayed love, one was met by indifference or flight.

The twins were thirteen years old and not identical. Saran, the elder by ten minutes, was small and slim, with dark hair curling over her head, and eyes the color of peat. Catrin was tall and coltish, with hair as red as Apple Falcon's had been, and a nose that turned up at the end in perpetual curiosity. Both were clad in dark bodices and red flannel skirts, their heads covered by knitted shawls.

"Did you bring the logs?" Mair demanded.

"All of them. I carried the most," Catrin said, plonking down on a stool with her knees apart and her head hanging as if she were posing for a tableau depicting "Exhaustion."

"That isn't so!" Saran said indignantly. "She simply makes more fuss about it."

"That will do, both of you!" Mair said sharply. "Catrin, have you done your lesson for the day?"

"Yes, Mam."

"Saran, the butter was not well churned this morning. You must use more vigor."

"Yes, Mam."

"You can pour yourselves some buttermilk," Mair said, relenting slightly.

"Can we have some bread?" Catrin, who was perpetually hungry, rolled her eyes pleadingly.

"One slice, or you'll spoil your supper." Mair took down her work basket and began to darn a pair of Catrin's stockings. "The holes in these are shameful. I think you eat the wool," she said.

"Is there fish for supper?" Saran asked hopefully.

"I bought some from Ianto Tanglenet. You can bring it out ready for frying."

Saran pulled open the door of the cupboard set in

the cool thickness of the stone wall. Mair preferred to keep fish there rather than in the dairy where the smell might taint the milk. It lay, its scales glinting with salt, in the plaited creel with leaves over it.

"Can I cook it, Mam?" Catrin, who was efficient at most household tasks, came over to her sister.

"You said I could make supper," Saran objected.

"Let Catrin do it, and you lay the table for me. And don't waste time in arguing."

Mair sighed, wincing as the point of the needle dug into her finger. Her hands were callous and red, with scorch marks across the palm of one where she had burnt it on a dish the previous week. She sucked the drop of blood and sighed again.

The evenings were the worst. During the day she could occupy herself with endless tasks, but when the twilight closed in and hid the brooding hills, then thoughts and memories rushed into her mind.

It was strange that she no longer clearly recalled Guto's narrow, dark face, but she could still see James clearly. So clearly that she sometimes felt that if she concentrated a little harder he would put out his hand and touch her. He must surely have guessed where she had fled, but not once in all the years had any enquiry been made for her. Occasionally, after a hard winter, she had considered the possibility of going back, of confessing the existence of the twins, of persuading him that she had not been responsible for the burning of the manor. But the impulse had always died. That James might believe her was probable. That he would forgive her infidelity and accept the twins was almost certain, but her pride shrank from the prospect of being forgiven.

It was of *Kingsmead*, too, that she thought of during the long evenings by the fire. She had never realized how closely her life was bound up in the great house where her ancestors had lived for three hundred years, nor how difficult it would be to return to the isolated farm where she had spent the first twenty years of her life; hard to renounce the comforts of genteel life, the unassuming presence of servants, the pretty clothes. All of these had become part of the fabric of her existence. Life in Saron was unrelenting and unyielding, measured by the seasons. The living she made from the land was a meager one, but she had reared the twins to be respectable, God-fearing girls, and not a breath of scandal had ever touched them. Her return, as a pregnant widow, had excited some comment, but in the years since she had lived solitary, seldom going down into the town, keeping herself purely to herself, discouraging any friendships between the twins and the other children on neighboring farmsteads.

"Mam, there's a paper here with a drawing of a castle on it," Saran said, delving into the creel. "It was under the fish. Is that where the King lives?"

Jerked back to the present, Mair held out a hand for the sheet of newspaper, the upper part of which depicted a line drawing of a battlemented courtyard with an arch against which a tree reared.

"Is it where the King lives?" Saran asked.

"No. No, it isn't." Mair answered automatically, the numbness of the shock chilling her limbs. Her eyes followed the close written paragraph beneath.

"*Kingsmead*, the charming residence of Lord James Falcon, was the scene of some considerable merriment recently when Lord Falcon's only surviving son, Nathan, was joined in holy matrimony to Miss Willow Clegg. Mr. Falcon's previous wife, Caroline, died tragically three months ago upon the birth of their son,

Harry. Readers will be aware that Lord Falcon has been closely connected with the new move towards social reform now current in ruling circles."

"It's the Court Gazette, isn't it?" Saran said, leaning on Mair's shoulder to read. "How did it get under the fish?"

"Ianto's wife sometimes buys an English newspaper," Mair said absently. "Go and help your sister. You can light the lamp if you wish."

Saran went obediently, and Mair began to fold up the papers, carefully, exactly, as if it were a vital task for her shaking fingers to perform.

So Nathan had married Caro, which meant that Caro had been saved from the fire. Probably Felice Browning had also been saved. No doubt she had been consoling James during the years of Mair's absence. But Caro had died, tragically according to the Court Gazette. And Nathan had married Willow Clegg. Nathan had married the bastard daughter of the woman James had once loved.

Moving as if in a dream, Mair went through into her bedroom. As bleakly furnished as the living room, its small window looked out over the sloping field. Under the sill a narrow chest held her changes of linen and the two fleecy shawls in which she had wrapped her babies.

She opened the lid and slid the paper inside. Numbness was tingling now into anger, a blind, bitter, unreasoning anger whose roots lay deep in the past.

Huldah Clegg had borne a child to James's brother, and that child had been a poison in the wine of Mair's happiness. She remembered the thin, pale, sly-eyed child who had continually intruded her presence into their lives. And now Willow Clegg was the future Lady Falcon, and would inherit—no, there was a

child. Caro had borne Nathan a son. A son called
Harry. That had been the name of the first Falcon,
the man to whom the land had been granted after
the dissolution of the monastery of Marie Regina.

The anger was so fierce that she felt as if she
were choking. She put a roughened hand up to the
neck of her dress and grimaced. The memory of Willow thickened the air. She leaned to fling open the
window and felt the cold air rush in, stinging her
face.

But the anger had hardened into a tight ball of
hatred, and its focus was Willow. Mair thought of her
still as a young girl, silent and secretive, moving
through the woods.

"The fish is ready, Mam," Catrin called from the
other room.

"You and Saran share it between you." Mair went
back into the living room. "I have to go out."

"It's nearly dark," Saran said.

"Nobody is going to run off with me," Mair said
tartly, pulling her shawl over her head.

As she went out into the yard she glanced back and
saw the two heads circled by lamplight, the black and
the red mingling together as they divided the fish.

Away from the yard she walked rapidly along the
broad track that led to the old well. She had discovered the dried-up well years before when she was
a child. It had been her secret place where she had
hidden when she had been avoiding a scolding for
some misdemeanor, or when she had been in one of
the dark moods that sometimes overcame her.

When Apple Falcon, her mother, lay dying, she had
given Mair the words of the curse, that curse passed
down in the Falcon family among the women who
bore the mark. Apple had been too sweet-natured to

wish harm to anyone, but she had complied with the tradition. And Mair had written down the words, written them down on a piece of paper, and put the paper in a little tin box, and thrown it down the old well.

That curse, never passed on by Mair, still existed and might even yet destroy Nathan's child as it had destroyed so many Falcons in the long years since a witch had come out of Wales to plant the tree at the arch of *Kingsmead*.

She had been walking too fast and the odd, choking sensation was in her throat again. But the tangle of bushes and trees that hid the abandoned well was in sight. She could discern them slanting against the purpling sky.

As she pushed her way into the center, thorns lashed at her face and tugged the strands of coarse grey hair that escaped her shawl. A spiteful wind was tossing the branches, snatching at her skirts, driving her breath back into her mouth when she opened it. Her head ached and the ball of anger inside her was a leaden weight.

The rim of the well was broken and crumbling. She reached it and leaned panting, staring down into the weed grown depths below. If she could only reach down and find it. The well had been half-silted up when she had originally thrown down the box.

The wind held its breath and a faint, first star danced above the horizon. Her arm ached and the leaden ball of hatred was growing bigger, then exploding, flaming into a thousand particles, each one aimed at her heart.

"I was never a bad woman," she said aloud into the stillness. "I loved James and I tried to make him happy. He was my husband, and my love should have been sufficient for him, but he had to be kind to all the world, had to spread his affection so thin that my own satisfaction was incomplete."

The pain filled her universe, and that universe was growing darker.

"You should take things more easily," Huw Postman Bach had said recently. "You're forever rushing around, Mrs. Price. Time to take it easy sometimes, you know."

"I'll rest when I've destroyed the words," she answered him now, but her own words were meaningless sounds gasped into the air, and the rim of the well cut into her sagging breast, and the moon mocked her lonely dying.

"Mam is in a black mood," Catrin said wisely as they scrubbed and dried the dishes together.

The twins were accustomed to those occasions when their mother, for no apparent reason, would tramp away through the fields and lanes and be gone long hours. The moods had something to do with their father, they guessed, though she never said as much. They had no idea of their father's name. He had died, Mair had told them, long before, when she had learned she was to bear a child.

"So I came back to my old home, to the place where I was born, and God sent me two babies instead of one. Perfect babes, without a mark on them," Mair had said, with a queer look of satisfaction on her face.

Catrin had ventured once to enquire, "Where were you living before we were born, Mam?" She had received a box on the ears to teach her not to be inquisitive, and gradually the desire to know more had faded from the girls' minds. They were aware only that they were, in some fashion, different. Their mother had taught them to read and write and to speak English, as well as to cook and sew and do the work of the farm. The education they had received and their own natures set them apart, for they had no need of other playmates to interrupt the games they played. Where Catrin went, Saran was never far behind.

"Shall we wait up or go to bed?" Saran asked her twin now.

"We'd better go to bed. Mam may be hours yet, and she'll not thank us for sitting up," Catrin advised.

"I'll leave the lamp burning low in the window," Saran said.

They went into their own bedroom after one last look into the yard in case their mother should be returning. But there was nothing to see save the black storm clouds rolling in from the marsh, nothing to hear save the rising of the wind.

They washed their hands and faces in the basin of cold water and dried them on the big towel they shared. Then Saran gave Catrin's unruly hair the required fifty strokes and Catrin, in turn, dealt with her sister's clustering curls. Finally, their clothes folded over the stool, their faces innocent above the high ruffles of their nightgowns, they knelt side by side to offer up their prayers.

"God bless Mam and us and keep us safe and the roof not leaking and the animals thriving and the crops healthy and the world at peace. Amen."

Catrin gabbled the prayers and jumped into the big bed, squealing as her bare feet met icy sheets. Saran said them more slowly, listening for her mother's step. Even when she had finished, instead of joining her twin, she drifted over to the window and stood, looking out into the dark field.

"Close the shutters and get into bed, do," Catrin said irritably.

"There's a blue flame, like a candle flame, far off in the mist," Saran said.

"Is it Mam coming with a lantern?"

"She didn't take one and there's only the flame. A blue flame. Come and see."

"It's a trick of the moon. Close the shutters," Catrin ordered sleepily.

"It looks like the death candle," Saran said.

"That's just a story," Catrin said, sitting up and hugging her knees. "Nobody believes it."

"Ieuan does. He told me that when someone of Welsh blood dies, a ghost flame hovers on the marsh."

"People die in Wales every day. The marshes ought to be lit up with ghost lights in that case," Catrin said briskly, lying down again. "Do close the shutters and come to bed!"

"It's gone now," Saran said.

"It was ever only in your mind," Catrin said.

"Sometimes the things in my mind seem more real than the things I can touch," Saran said fearfully.

There was no answer from the bed beyond an impatient snort and, after a moment, Saran padded over to join her twin.

James leaned his head on his hand and sighed. It was becoming increasingly difficult to sleep, though he rose at dawn and worked every hour of the day. But he was troubled by constant insomnia and by a gnawing pain in his stomach that came on him after he had eaten. The pains had begun shortly after Nathan's second marriage and showed no signs of abating, though Willow was sweetness itself, forever persuading him to try this or that of the herbal mixtures she concocted.

On this evening his spirits were particularly low. His head ached, the pain in his stomach had begun to nag again, his eyes were tired. He had had a glass of port, but the liquid, instead of comforting, had scorched his throat.

He leaned back in his chair and looked tiredly about the great hall. It was old and shabby in the light of the candles, the tapestries faded and patched, the flagstones worn. From the gallery the faces of his ancestors looked down.

His life, he thought drearily, had been a sham, a hollow failure. The first girl he had ever loved had turned instead to his brother; his wife had rejected him and left. Not a day passed when he did not think of her, calling her image to his mind so strongly that when he opened his eyes he almost expected to see her standing there. But she was never there, and the hopefulness sank into despair again, for if any love for him remained in her heart, she would surely have returned.

In the bedroom over the kitchen Nathan stood looking down at his six-months-old son. It was not often that he had the opportunity to be alone with the child, for Willow was so devoted to the babe that she seldom let him out of her sight.

Harry was outgrowing his early delicacy. A sturdy babe, with his mother's blue eyes and a mop of nut-brown hair, he had already begun to pull himself into a standing position. When he smiled, which was often, two white teeth gleamed in the pinkness of his gums. He was asleep now, nestled in blankets.

"My son," Nathan said, and reached out to touch his cheek.

From the doorway Willow said, "Please, Nathan,

don't wake him up! I had a terrible task getting him to sleep."

"You should leave him to Betsy sometimes," Nathan said.

"Betsy is clumsy," Willow said. "Don't move that lamp."

"I wasn't going to," Nathan said mildly.

"The light disturbs him if it shines in his eyes," Willow said, as if he had not spoken. "Come into the sitting room. I want to show you something."

He went, with one last, loving glance at the tousled, sleeping head.

The sitting room was cool and quiet and serene. As usual Nathan had the sense of being underwater when he entered. The pale greens and silvers of the furnishings suited Willow. Caro, for whom the room had been prepared, had been too bright, too full of sparkling chatter, to fit into the dreamy pastel scheme.

"I never intended to disturb the babe," he began.

"You did not disturb him. Sit down, do."

He sat cautiously, wondering what new fault she had to find. He could never accuse her of bad temper. It was simply that she pointed out his shortcomings plaintively and sweetly, and when he had admitted to them, and apologized for them, she sometimes allowed him to make love to her.

"I have been neglectful of you these past weeks," she said, surprisingly.

"The babe is teething." He offered her her own excuse for having rejected him five times out of six.

"But I am apt to worry too much about his welfare. It is simply that I would not have people call me indifferent to poor Caro's child."

"You are an excellent mother," he said warmly.

"And I do think of you," she said, with a little catch in her voice. "I have been writing a poem for you."

"A poem! I didn't know that you ever wrote poems."

"It is not very good," she said. "Would you like me to say it for you?"

"Yes. Yes, I would."

She stood like a child, her small hands clasped behind her wide green skirts, her pale face upraised as if she waited for a blow or a kiss. Her voice fell, cool and silvery into the green room.

> If you go first, will you wait for me
> In the land where there is no time?
> Will you keep faith with the vow we vowed
> And still be mine?
> If I go first, will you follow me
> Swift and sure and believing still?
> Never draw back and leave me there
> On the darkling hill?
> Seedtime was short and the harvest late
> And winter has frozen the swallow's lament,
> But the words I spoke as you entered my gate
> Were truly meant.

"My love, that was beautiful." Deeply moved, Nathan would have put his arms about her, but she evaded him, her mouth curved into a regretful smile.

"I am so weary tonight," she murmured. "Forgive me if I slip out for a breath of air. Why don't you sit with your father for a while? He is not at all well."

"I'll go down to him." He blew a kiss and went out onto the gallery.

She waited for a few minutes, secure in the muted fastness of her sitting-room. When she descended the stairs the great hall was empty, but she could hear the faint murmur of voices from the solar.

She opened the front door and stepped out quietly into the courtyard. Her low heels made no sound on the cobbles as she went toward the archway, beyond which the luck-tree guarded the wall.

She reached up and plucked some of the leaves, crushing them and inhaling their vinegary scent. The moon emerging from behind the trees struck fire from the black stone, set now in a ring of gold.

"An opal," Nathan had said. "A very fine, black opal. Where did you get it?"

"There were some stones for sale in the jewellers' at Maidstone," she had answered vaguely.

Now, holding her hand up to the pale light, she whispered in triumph. "I have it all now. Caro's husband, Caro's babe, the gypsy's stone. It's all mine, and nobody will ever snatch it away from me. Nobody! You and I, Lilith, have won, and taken what we wanted." Somewhere, deep inside her, in that uncorrupted part of herself where her affections lay, a voice whispered, cold and clear, *"Take what you want, and pay."* For a moment the moonlight and the arching tree threatened her. Then she lifted her chin, slanting her eyes, and smiled, for the day of reckoning was not yet come.

THE END